W9-ATY-583

BUT WHAT ABOUT ME?

Also by Marilyn Reynolds:

Telling

Detour for Emmy

Too Soon for Jeff

Beyond Dreams

BUT WHAT ABOUT ME?

Marilyn Reynolds

Morning
Glory
Press

Buena Park, California

Library of Congress Cataloging-in-Publication Data
Reynolds, Marilyn, 1935-
    But what about me? / Marilyn Reynolds.
      p.   cm. -- (True-to-life series from Hamilton High)
Summary: Erica has always been a serious student but
when her boyfriend's life starts spinning out of control, she
does not anticipate the tragic consequences his behavior
could have on her future.
    ISBN 1-885356-11-0 (hc). -- ISBN 1-885356-10-2 (pbk.)
    [1. Conduct of life--Fiction. 2. High schools--Fiction.
3. Schools--Fiction.] I. Title. II. Series: Reynolds,
Marilyn, 1935-   True-to-life stories from Hamilton High.
PZ7.R3373Bu   1996
[Fic]--dc20   96-23108
                                                          CIP
                                                          AC

MORNING GLORY PRESS, INC.
6595 San Haroldo Way   Buena Park, CA 90620
Telephone 714/828-1998
FAX 714/828-2049
Printed and bound in the United States of America

I feel him heavy on top of me, grabbing at my jeans.

"You think you're somethin'. You ain't nothin'," he says, breathing stale whiskey into my face.

"Get away from me! Get off!"

I buck hard, trying to move him, grab his hair to get his ugly face off mine. Where's Danny?

"Danny!" I scream. "Danny!"

"He ain't gonna help you now."

Acknowledgments

I wish to thank:

Sandy DeMarco and Michael Quinlan of the Pasadena Humane Society, and also Danielle Chapman, Windy Wilde and Kristy-Lynn Surbida who are volunteers with that most humane organization.

Busy people from the Pasadena YWCA Rape Crisis Center and the Los Angeles County Juvenile Justice Center who were willing to spend telephone time answering questions.

Century High School students who've offered their own particular insights along the way.

My writing/critiquing cohorts, David Doty, Toni Frank, Karen Kasaba, Deborah Lott, Danny Miller, Anne Scott, and Lynne Shook.

The Morning Glory Press crew.

Mimi Avocada.

Marilyn Reynolds

To Mike

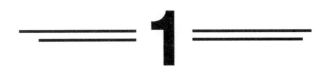
The first time I ever talked to Danny Lara was about a year ago, at the Humane Society where I work. He and his friend, Alex, were both seniors at Hamilton High School and they needed to complete the Community Service requirement for graduation, so they'd signed up as volunteers. It was a Wednesday afternoon near the end of October.

I was a junior at the time. I'd seen Alex and Danny around school, but I didn't know them. The reason I can still remember it was late October is because we weren't letting any black cats be adopted out. That's one of the rules—no black cats go out the week before Halloween, and no rabbits go out the week before Easter. Animals are not meant to be used for decorative purposes is the way Sinclair Manchester, the director of the volunteer program, explains those rules.

On that particular day, Sinclair was busy getting volunteers set up to help with a mobile pet adoption trip to the mall, so he asked me to help Danny and Alex.

"Get them started socializing with the dogs," he'd said.

I love Sinclair. He's this energetic, wiry black guy, probably about thirty. He has his official Humane Society shirts custom tailored and sends them to a special hand laundry. According to Dr. Franz, the veterinarian, Sinclair is definitely the best dressed Humane Society employee in the nation.

"Do you think we could organize a national S.P.C.A. fashion show?" Sinclair asked one day, walking to the end of a row of cages, then turning a model style turn and striking a pose. Besides being a great boss, Sinclair keeps everyone laughing.

Anyway, that day last October, Alex and Danny came walking downstairs, wearing their volunteer name badges on red H.H.H.S. (Hamilton Heights Humane Society) smocks and carrying their kennel keys.

Alex was tall and very thin, with blond hair that looked like he never washed or combed it. He had a tiny silver ring in his right eyebrow. Danny was taller, nearly six feet, I guessed, and darker. But he wasn't skinny like Alex. Definitely not fat, either, but muscular.

They stopped at the big cage where the caracara bird lives. According to the information card, he's a cross between a rooster and a falcon wearing a toupee. "Toopee" is the staff's nickname for him.

"Look at his colors," Danny said.

"Cool," Alex said. "He's got a black flat top and his face is all orange, like he's used some phony tanning lotion."

"He was rescued from a house up in Sycamore Hills. They found him all cramped up in a cage not much bigger than a shoe box," I told them.

"Rich people," Alex says, spitting the hate-filled words out.

"Neighbors called about it. It's totally illegal to have one of these birds. They're endangered."

Suddenly the bird threw its head back and made a warbling, piercing sound.

"Wow!" Alex said. "Did you see that?"

Danny's eyes were wide with surprise. It *is* an amazing sight. When the bird calls out like that, its head reaches all the way down its back, like it's folded with its throat totally exposed.

After they watched the caracara for awhile I led them to the section where the dogs needed socialization. That's the first job volunteers get—socialization—which just means spending some time with a particular dog, petting it, playing with it, sometimes taking it out to the dirt yard so it can run around.

"You can pick any dog with a green dot on its identification card," I said.

I took the disinfectant spray bottle and sprayed the soles of my shoes, then passed it to Alex.

Everybody has to have three Saturday training sessions before they can actually work with the animals, so I expected those guys to know the routine. I was surprised when Alex pushed the bottle back at me.

"I don't need that," he said. He unlocked the gate of a pen that held a big, brown mutt who was frantically wagging her tail and whining for attention.

Alex opened the gate. I slammed it shut.

"Whoa," Danny said with a laugh. "Don't mess with her."

"You *do* need it," I said, shoving the bottle back at Alex.

"What're you? Queen of the kennels?"

"What're you? An imbecile?"

Alex put the key into the lock.

"Spray first," I told him.

"I'm not afraid of a few germs."

Again he opened the gate.

Again, I slammed it shut. The poor dog was going nuts, getting her hopes up with each turn of the key and having them dashed with each slamming of the gate.

"You don't spray your shoes to keep *you* germ free," I said. "It's for the animals, so you don't spread any diseases from one to the other."

"Just spray your shoes, man," Danny said, taking the bottle from Alex and spraying the soles of his own shoes.

"Here," Danny said. "That guy, Sinclair, already told us all about this. Just do it."

"I don't have to do what some black girly-man says."

I stiffened. I *hate* when people put other people down, just because they're different.

"Sinclair's one of the nicest people in the world," I said, feeling my face go hot.

"Yeah, for a faggot," Alex said, laughing.

"That's cold," I said.

"You're out of line, Homes," Danny said. "Just spray your shoes."

Alex gave a little laugh and sprayed his shoes.

"Don't mind him," Danny said. "He's only messing around."

I watched outside the pen while Danny and Alex knelt down next to the brown dog. I didn't really trust them. Alex started rubbing the dog behind the ears, talking to her in a gentle voice I'd not heard earlier. The brown dog obviously liked him. Maybe he wasn't all bad.

Later that evening when I was talking on the phone to my friend, April, I asked if she knew Danny Lara and Alex Kendall.

"Yeah, they're cool," she'd said.

"Alex is an idiot."

"His family's all messed up."

"How?"

"I hear his mom's kind of an alcoholic. And his older brother's in some Youth Authority camp for assault, or robbery, or something."

"Nice people," I said, sarcastically.

"Alex is okay," April said. "He's practically grown up at Danny's house."

"Where do you come up with all this information?"

"I just pay attention," she'd said. "Besides, I've lived in this place lots longer than you have."

"Also, you're a big gossip," I reminded her.

"It's career training," she said.

April wants to be one of those talk show people, like Courtney Case or Ricki Lake. She thought she had a natural talent for gossip. Our career ed teacher told her to be a natural gossip was a curse, not a talent, but April didn't see it that way.

As I told April how Danny had managed to smooth things over, and how he'd later calmed a dog that had been all scared and shivery, I realized I was sort of going on and on about Danny Lara.

"Sounds like love to me," she'd said, jumping to one of her famous, unfounded conclusions.

"You're an idiot, too," I told her, laughing. It turns out the laugh was on me, which April reminds me of every chance she gets.

When Danny showed up in the dog kennel the following week, he went straight for the spray bottles. Then he came down to the puppy section, where I'd just cleaned a pen and was playing with five black puppies who had white feet and white muzzles. He walked into the pen where I was working, then leaned down and scratched the back of one of the pups.

"I'm sorry about the other day," Danny said with a smile. It was the first time I'd noticed the dimple in his right cheek, or that his eyes were sort of a light hazel color. "Alex really doesn't mean any harm."

"I don't like hearing people make fun of Sinclair," I said, getting mad again just thinking about Alex's attitude.

"Hey," Danny said, holding his hands up in a gesture of surrender, "I didn't say anything bad about Sinclair. Don't get mad at me."

We both laughed.

"They had to put down some dogs about a year ago, because of a disease that spread through the kennels. It was really sad," I told him.

"And cats, too, I heard."

"Yeah, that happened back before I worked here, before the new addition. Now there's enough distance between the cages that the cats can't sneeze on each other anymore."

"Cool," Danny said.

I looked at him carefully, to see if he was making fun of me.

"No, really. That's cool. I like how careful they are with all the animals in this place."

"The hardest thing about working here is knowing that sometimes animals are put to death, just because nobody wants them, and they've got to make room for more animals coming in," I said.

"They should just let them loose when that happens. Give them a chance."

"No. You should see what happens to strays. That's no life—half-starving, mangy, maybe getting hit by a car, no one to protect them or love them."

Danny followed me out of the black puppies' pen. We resprayed our shoes and washed our hands, and then went into the next pen, which had a mix of eight pups, some black, some brown. I started the cleaning routine while the pups clamored over my feet and rubbed at my legs.

"Don't you mind cleaning puppy poop all the time?" Danny asked.

"No—I've been doing it so long, it's no worse than any other dirt to me now."

Danny made a face, then filled the bowl with fresh water.

"Where *is* your friend today, anyway?"

"Alex doesn't want to come back. You scared him."

"No."

"Well, not really. He had to take his mom somewhere today."

"Have you been friends a long time?"

"Since kindergarten."

"I wonder what it would be like, to have a friend since kindergarten."

"Don't you?"

"No. My dad's in the army and we moved around a lot. My friend April . . ."

"April Williams?"

"Yeah, she's the first friend I've ever had for more than two years. I met her in the eighth grade, when we first moved to Hamilton Heights."

"Have you stopped moving around now?" Danny asked.

"My parents bought a house here. My dad's retiring in a few years."

We went on like that, talking and cleaning the pens and playing with the dogs until it was time to leave.

"Which days do you come in?" Danny asked me.

"It varies. Right now I'm here on Mondays, Wednesdays, and Saturday afternoons."

"Well, me too, then," he said. "Do you usually work with the pups?"

"I start with them, but sometimes I'm in the infirmary, assisting with inoculations, or with spaying and neutering."

"You assist?"

"Well, I prep the animals—shave them and disinfect the area, that kind of thing . . . I want to be a vet, so this is great experience for me—also it will look good on my college applications."

Danny groaned.

"What?"

"College applications. I've got to start thinking about that stuff."

"Where do you want to go?"

"Maybe Cal Poly. I don't have a clue about what I want to be, though. My mom thinks I should do something in environmental studies because I'm constantly nagging them about recycling."

"Environmental studies might be good," I said. "You'd be doing something important."

"I don't know. All I know for sure is I don't want to end up in construction like my dad. He works his butt off and now he's all worried about getting old and not being able to keep up."

We walked out by the horned owl's cage. He looked at us like he knew something we didn't.

"He's amazing," Danny said. "Too bad he's caged in."

"He was rescued last summer. One of his wings was all messed up. They always try to return wild animals to their natural habitat, but this one will never be able to survive on his own again. He can't fly well enough to get his own food."

We went to another puppy pen—a litter of seven little mongrels.

"I like helping with the spaying and neutering," I told Danny. "Every animal neutered means fewer unwanted animals to be euthanized."

"Euthanized?"

"You know. Put to sleep."

We left the pen, sprayed our shoes again, washed our hands, then went to a pen with a funny looking little dog in it—a kind of shepherd/dachshund mix.

"Wow. Look at you," Danny said, laughing at the dog.

She rolled over on her back and looked up at him with pleading eyes. Danny rubbed her chest.

"Look," I pointed to the card on the pen. "She's been adopted."

"Lucky doggie," Danny said, "Lucky, lucky dog."

Before Danny left that day he told me, "See you Wednesday."

I'd always been happy on Humane Society days, partly because I felt like I was doing something important, and partly because I always had a favorite animal to look forward to seeing. Then, after Danny started showing up the same days I was there, I was doubly, or maybe triply, happy on Humane Society days.

By the time he'd completed his Community Service requirement, some time before Christmas last year, Danny and I were seeing each other every day at school, and hanging around together on weekends, and April's unfounded conclusion of "sounds like love to me" had come true.

I don't want to get all sentimental here, but that was a very happy time for me, back when Danny and I first got together, when things were still going well for him. I hope things start going well for him again, like they did before his mom died. She was all happy one minute, making plans for a big family reunion-type eighteenth birthday party for Danny. The next minute she was hit by a car as she crossed the street to a nursery and garden supply place.

Danny's changed a lot since the accident. I know a person doesn't get over something like that overnight, though. Sometimes he looks so sad—more than anything I want to be there for him, love him through the sad times—just like I know he would love me through the sad times if things were the other way around.

2

"**E**rica! Telephone!" Mom yells from the kitchen.

I set the biology study guide on top of my open textbook and walk quickly out of my bedroom. Finally! Danny said he'd call at six, and it's already after eight. It gets me annoyed when he does that. I try to concentrate on studying, but mainly what I end up doing is wondering why Danny hasn't called. And worrying.

Mom is just out of the shower, wearing her ratty terrycloth robe, drying her hair with a thick, purple towel. Her hair is black, like mine, but super short. It only takes about five minutes for her to dry it. When I'm thirty-eight, like my mom is now, I'll probably have short hair like that, too. For now though, at almost eighteen, I like my hair long. Danny likes my hair long. He says it's lavishly luscious. That makes the thirty-minute drying time worth the effort.

Mom holds the phone out for me with her free hand.

My ten-year-old sister, Rochelle (Rocky for short), jumps up and down. "I'll bet it's your husband," she says.

"Don't be so silly," Mom says, handing me the phone.

"Erica's married, Erica's married," Rochelle sings.

"Rocky's jealous," I say, mimicking her tone.

Ever since Rocky first met Danny, when I started going around with him a year ago, she's had this huge crush on him.

I take the phone back to my bedroom. There's no such thing as privacy around my nosy little sister, but at least we finally got a cordless phone. Before that I had to talk in the kitchen where Sister Big Ears and my mom could hear every word.

"Erica, wait'll you hear this! It's so sad."

My heart sinks. I was sure it would be Danny but instead it's April. I mean, I want to talk to April and all. But I've been waiting for Danny to call for the past two hours.

"What? Hear what?" I ask.

"Remember that girl who thought she was so tough—you know, the spike queen on the Whitman volleyball team?"

"The really tall one?" I ask, trying to figure out who she's talking about.

"Yeah, with the streaked purple hair."

"Sandra?"

"Yeah, that's her name. She's got AIDS."

"AIDS?"

"Yeah. For reals."

"How do you know?" I ask. April finds more sensational stories than that talk show woman, Courtney Case.

"You know Brett? In Peer Counseling? She told me."

"How does Brett know?"

"They're cousins. Remember when Ms. Woods was telling us about those AIDS Center people who are coming to talk to our class?"

"Yeah. Tomorrow, right?"

"I think so. Anyway, Brett told me about how her cousin just tested positive for HIV. Brett's *all* upset because she was the one who set her cousin up with this guy."

I remember Sandra from the volleyball play-offs. She was quick and strong and tireless.

"Testing positive doesn't mean she's got AIDS," I say.

"She's only seventeen and her life is already over," April says.

"You *always* exaggerate," I accuse April.

"And you *never* face things," April accuses back.

"Always, never," I say.

We laugh. In Peer Counseling we've worked on clear, non-judgmental communication. Among other things, that means avoiding statements like "you never," or "you always," and sticking to "I" statements rather than "you" statements.

"So . . ." April says.

"So . . . I feel it's an exaggeration to assume that Sandra's life is over, based on the rumor that she's tested positive for HIV," I say, trying to come up with an "I" statement.

"And *I* feel that it is an act of denial to assume that Sandra will have any kind of life with HIV."

I've been friends with April since we were on the volleyball team at Palm Avenue School back in the eighth grade. We argue all the time, but we never really get angry with one another. Maybe a little irritated, but not angry.

"Wouldn't you think your life was over if you tested HIV positive?" April asks. "Or would you be expecting some Disney happy ending to come from it?"

"I wouldn't test positive," I say.

"I know. But just what if?"

April *loves* to talk about what if kinds of things. I prefer reality.

A quick buzz lets me know there's a call waiting.

"I'll call you back, April. Okay?"

"Okay. Make it quick though. My dad's going to take me out for a driving lesson as soon as he gets home."

I hang up and the next call comes in. This time it's Danny.

"Hey, Pups," he says.

That's Danny's nickname for me—Pups. He started calling me that when we worked together at the Humane Society. He claimed he could always find me around the puppy kennels—just look for the pups and Erica will be there, he said.

It sounds stupid to other people, I guess, but I like that Danny cared enough from the very beginning to make up a nickname for me.

Even though it's lots later than he said he'd call, something in me melts at the sound of Danny's voice.

"Hi, Dan," I say, leaning back in my chair, my feet resting on the table next to the experimental protocol for identifying introns in RNA processing. I'm ready for a long talk about anything but biology.

"What's up?" Danny asks.

"I'm trying to study for a big bio test tomorrow. I desperately need an *A* on this one."

"You could lighten up on the school stuff. A *B* wouldn't hurt now and then."

"Tell that to UC Davis," I say.

"I can't believe you'll be going away in August," Danny says.

"It seems like a long way away."

"Nine months. That's not really very long," Danny says.

Kitty, my big golden retriever, lies heavy on my bare feet, keeping them warm. I reach down to pet her and she turns over on her back, legs spread, inviting me to rub her belly. I've had her for five years, since she was a puppy. Her name shows what a weird sense of humor I had in junior high school. I named her Kitty just to confuse people. It really is funny to see the expressions on people's faces when I call, "Here, Kitty, Kitty, Kitty," and this giant dog comes running to me.

I rub Kitty's soft underside absentmindedly.

"You might forget me when you get up there with all those college boys," Danny says.

"Never," I tell him. "You're my first and only love."

"For really truly?" he says.

"For really truly."

I stroke Kitty's silky golden hair. There is a lot of noise from Danny's end of the line.

"Where are you?" I ask, knowing his dad told him to stay home tonight.

"Nowhere," he says.

"Where's that?" I say.

He just laughs. "Around the corner from Somewhere."

"Where are you really?"

"C'mon, Pups," he says. "I called to talk to you, not be put on the stand."

In the background someone says "Hey, Dude, pass it along," and I know Danny is at Alex's house—the party house.

"I thought you were staying home tonight."

"I was, but then my dad started raggin' on me. I can't take it there anymore. I'm moving in with Alex for awhile, just 'til I can get my own place."

"Is it okay with Alex's mom?"

"Yeah, she doesn't care one way or the other."

I've only met Alex's mom once, but I hear she's the biggest partier of all. That would be so weird, to have a mom like that.

"There are so many people in and out of this place, she'll hardly notice I'm there. Besides, Alex owes me."

"Why?"

"He used to always stay at my place, to get away from his nutcase brother. That was before Joey got sent to camp, and before my mom died . . . Listen, why don't I come see you after awhile?"

"You know how my mom is about you coming over on a school night. It's like I'm still Rochelle's age."

"How about after your mom goes to bed? . . . I miss you," he says, in that low tone of voice that always gets to me.

"I don't know. We almost got caught last time."

There is a long pause. Then Danny says in a whisper, "I feel so lonely sometimes, Pups. You're the only one who makes things better."

No one has ever needed me the way Danny needs me, or loved me the way Danny loves me. I mean, my parents love me and all, but I'm talking about a grown-up, romantic kind of love.

"Erica? I want so much to feel you next to me."

A familiar warmth spreads through my body.

"I'll leave my window unlocked."

"I'll be so quiet Kitty won't even hear me."

"Rochelle's the one I'm worried about," I tell him. "I don't think my spying sister ever sleeps."

"Be waiting for me. Remember I love you," Danny says.

I hear a noise on the phone.

"I know you just picked up the phone, Rochelle! Hang up now!" I yell, totally breaking the mood, but what can I do?

"I have to call Jessica about my homework," she whines. "You've been on the phone forever and now it's my turn!"

"Hey, Rocky," Danny says, "Just hang up and we'll be off the phone in a minute."

"Okay. 'Bye, Danny," she says, suddenly sounding all sweet and innocent. I hear a click of the receiver and know Rocky hung up.

"So I'll see you after the lights go out," Danny says.

He taps the phone receiver three times, meaning "I love you." I tap back four times, meaning "I love you, too," and we hang up. I take the phone back to the kitchen and put it in front of my sister, who is still at the table doing fifth grade math. I wish my homework were as easy as hers.

"I know what you were talking about," she chants.

"What?"

"Love stuff."

"You watch too much TV," I tell her.

"No, I don't. Mom never lets me watch TV."

"Because you never get your homework done."

"Because you never help me. Because you're always busy talking to your *husband* on the phone."

I look over her shoulder at her homework and work out a division problem for her. I should go right back to my room, and biology, but instead I reach for Kitty's leash. Maybe a short run will clear my mind, so I can study better. At least now I can stop worrying about Danny, now that I know he'll be climbing through my window late tonight.

Kitty runs to the back door, then back to me, toenails clicking on the kitchen floor. She goes into a slide, ending at my feet.

"Wanna go for a run, Kitty?" I say in a voice that I know will excite her even more. "Wanna run?"

Kitty runs again to the door, makes a circle through the house, down the hall, through the living room, then a full slide through the kitchen, and finally back to the door where she zips around in circles, chasing her tail. Rocky and I, as always, laugh hysterically at Kitty's antics. Mom glances up from the catalog she's been looking through.

"That dog is going to be the ruin of this house," she says, but she's smiling. No one can watch Kitty carry on like that without at least smiling.

My mom never really wanted a dog. She said they were dirty and carried fleas and they were too much trouble. Before, when we'd lived with my dad on army bases, there was always a no pets rule, so there was no way we could have a dog. "If only we had our own place," Mom would say, "then you could have a dog." So when we moved to our house in Hamilton Heights, my mom didn't have any more excuses. We went to the Humane Society the day after we moved in here.

My parents decided I should have a more normal high school experience than the army brat life I'd always lived, and they were worried because Rochelle was turning into some kind of wild child. Also, my grampa had just died, and my gramma was all alone. Plus she had diabetes, so my mom was worried about her. So we had one of those big family conferences in which the parents do all the talking.

"Dad and I always planned to live in Hamilton Heights after his retirement. The three of us will just get settled early."

"I'll miss all of my girls," Dad said, holding Mom's hand. "But it's the right thing. Your education is important, and Hamilton School District has much more to offer than you can get from any overseas school."

"It will help Gramma, too, to have us nearby," Mom said.

So my mom and Rochelle and I settled down in Hamilton Heights, in Southern California, where my mom grew up. We just see Dad a couple of times a year now, when he comes home on a long leave. That part is hard. But it's good to get out of that cycle: make new friends—move; make new friends—move. Over and over again. I hated that. By the time I was in the sixth grade, it hardly seemed worth the effort to make new friends, knowing we'd be moving again anytime.

Besides running out of reasons why we couldn't get a dog, I think Mom worried about how much we'd all miss Dad, and hoped a dog would take our minds off our loneliness. I thought it would help if we named our new dog Daddy, but they wouldn't go for that. I'm glad now. She's a perfect Kitty.

We got Kitty when she was still a pup. Her mom had an affair with a German shepherd, so she's not a total golden retriever. Kitty was the runt of the litter. Not only did I fall in love with Kitty that day, back when I was thirteen, I fell in love with the Humane Society. As soon as I was old enough, fourteen, I became a volunteer, and then, last year, they hired me part-time, for money. A job at the Humane Society is perfect for me because I want to be a vet.

When we got Kitty, my mom and dad had wanted us to get one of the other pups instead, saying maybe Kitty wouldn't be as healthy as her bigger brothers and sisters. But Kitty and I had already bonded the minute she looked up at me with her big, gentle eyes. I knew beyond a doubt that she was the pup for me.

Rocky, who was only six at the time, didn't care which dog we got, as long as we got a dog. Even though Kitty is supposed to be Rocky's dog too, she's more mine because I was the person who chose her and I take care of her.

Kitty stands still long enough for me to attach the leash to her collar, then pulls toward the door.

"I wanna go," Rochelle says.

"Come on then."

Rochelle starts jumping around again. Sometimes that's how she expresses herself, by jumping—sort of like Kitty. She's as hyper as Kitty, too, running after me whenever I even *think* about going anywhere. Not only that, but Rochelle's hair is practically the same color as Kitty's, a deep, rusty red that shines brown and blond in the sunlight. Come to think of it, Rocky's about the same height as Kitty. When Kitty stands on her hind legs she's about shoulder height on me. That's how tall Rocky is, too, when *she* stands on her hind legs. My sister the dog. My dog the kitty. Weird.

Mom leans over the round oak table that sits in what the real estate person called a dining area, but what is really just the far end of our kitchen. It's the table where we have dinner, and where Rochelle does her homework, and where Mom pays the bills. I used to do my homework here, too, but now I prefer my bedroom. It's quieter. And sometimes I have a lot to think about besides homework, and my bedroom's a better place to do that than at the big oak table where my mom sometimes pulls up a chair and says, a penny for your thoughts. I don't always want to share my thoughts.

"You haven't done even half of your math problems, Rochelle," Mom says.

"I'll finish when I get back," Rochelle says. "It's only nine."

"I want you in bed, homework finished, by ten at the latest."

Rochelle jumps up and down again, kisses Mom, and follows me and Kitty out the door. I jog at a slow pace, so Rochelle can keep up. Her legs are so much shorter than mine, she practically has to take two steps to my one.

We run up Primrose to Solano, then to Canyon Crest, where the houses are twice as big as the one we live in.

We stop for a minute while I unhook Kitty's leash. I'm not supposed to let her off the leash, but she always comes right back when I call her, so I let her run free where it's safe. I love to watch her run, with her legs fully stretched out and her silky, bronze hair blown back by the breeze she creates. I wish we lived in the country, with no fences, so she could run like that whenever she feels like it.

Rochelle and I walk for awhile, not talking. It's strange. At home, in front of our mom, Rochelle is constantly bugging me. But when we're out like this, with Kitty, she's more like a friend than a pesty little sister. That's how she is when I pick her up from her after-school choir practices, too. But at home? She's a brat.

"Do you think that girl really has AIDS?" she says.

"Rocky! Were you listening in on Mom's bedroom phone again?"

"No," she says, all indignant, like she'd never even consider such a thing. "I heard *you*. You practically yelled it. '*AIDS?*' you yelled, and you said something about someone named Sandra. I can't help it if you yell into the phone."

"Oh, man. I told April I'd call her right back and I totally forgot," I say. "Here, Kitty, Kitty, Kitty," I call. Kitty slides to a stop, turns, and comes racing back to me.

"Do you?" Rochelle says.

"Do I what?"

"Do you think that girl has AIDS?"

"I don't know," I say. "I think April is making another of her colossal leaps to an unfounded conclusion."

"Speak English, please," Rochelle says.

"Develop a vocabulary, please," I say, laughing.

I attach Kitty's leash and we jog back to the house. I call April as soon as I get home, but I only reach her machine. April has her *own* private phone number and her *own* answering machine, which is what I'm saving my money for—that, and Christmas presents.

The Humane Society pays minimum wage, and I only work

twelve hours a week, so saving money is a slow process. I'm hoping that when my dad gets home for his Christmas leave, he'll match what I already have saved and help me get my phone and answering machine. Sometimes I can work deals with my dad that my mom would never go for. Especially like during the first week or so, when Dad is still outrageously happy to see us.

3

I don't want to still be grossly sweaty from jogging when Danny gets here, so I take a quick shower, then get into a fresh T-shirt and sweats. I stand in front of the bathroom mirror, brushing the dampness from my hair. My hair is my best feature, I guess—thick and shiny and healthy looking, with just enough natural wave to be interesting. The rest of me is average through and through—average size, average height, average nose, dark eyes—April is always trying to talk me into getting light green contacts. You'd look *way* cool if you'd do that, she tells me. I'm sure! I'm hardly the type to go around sticking foreign objects in my eyes, no matter how cool April thinks I'd look.

Rocky and I don't look the least bit like sisters. She takes after my German grampa as far as coloring goes. When I first started high school, I wished I was light, like Rocky. It seemed more glamorous. But Danny's always telling me how beautiful my dark eyes are, and how much he loves my thick black hair, so now I'm happier with the way I look.

I reach for the lotion and rub a generous portion into my hands. At work, I'm constantly washing my hands, so my skin is super dry. Dr. Franz says I'd better plan on that for life if I'm going to be a vet.

Dr. Franz has been a kind of mentor to me. When I first started volunteering here, it was because I wanted to be around the animals. But after I saw how important it was that they be spayed and neutered, and vaccinated, I started thinking about being a vet.

Gradually, Dr. Franz taught me how to prepare animals for surgery, mix vaccines, and use the centrifuge as part of the blood testing process. On work days at the Humane Society, first I check with Dr. Franz, to see what's needed with the health team, and, if they don't need me, I work with Sinclair. He's my official boss, but most of the time I'm with the health team. It's amazing how much I've learned at the Humane Society.

Speaking of learning, I *must* study for my biology test.

Biology's pretty easy, if I concentrate, but I'm not like Phillip or Gabrielle, who can practically just glance at the cover of the book and know everything inside it. Doing well in science classes is really important to me because becoming a veterinarian is almost as hard as becoming a regular doctor. Really, there are fewer veterinarian schools in the country than there are medical schools, so in some ways it's even *harder* to become a vet.

I go over the test checklist and start rereading things I don't yet understand very well. Identification of exons and introns, and RNA processing, is still a mystery to me. I'm just beginning to get a glimmer of understanding when Mom comes to the door with the phone.

"Danny's dad," she says.

I take the phone from her.

"Hello?"

"Erica?"

"Yes," I say, wondering why Mr. Lara would be calling me.

"Is Daniel with you?"

"No."

"I told him not to leave the house tonight but the minute I turned my back he was gone."

Mr. Lara sounds very angry. I don't know what to say.

"Do you know where he is?"

"Not really," I say.

"What do you mean, not really?"

"I'm not sure where Danny is—sorry," I say.

"Well, when you see him, tell him to get his butt home. I'm waiting for him."

"Okay," I say, and hang up.

I didn't *exactly* lie to Mr. Lara. I mean, Danny never told me where he was when he called, but I knew anyway. But if I'd said Danny was at Alex's his dad would have gone nuts. He's always accusing Danny of being a low life and he hates the guys who hang out at Alex's.

I go back to RNA processing, but I can't concentrate. I'm reading the same stuff over and over again, all the time thinking about how mad Mr. Lara sounded and what big trouble Danny's in. His dad's already threatened to kick Danny out of the house if he doesn't change his ways.

On Danny's eighteenth birthday, only a few weeks after his mother died, Danny's dad told him, "You're an adult now—time to pull your own load. Don't think you can keep living off me."

I really worry about Danny. I love him so much, I don't ever want him to be hurt, or in trouble. Danny's dad is always angry with him because he's not working and he hasn't graduated from high school yet. He just quit going to school when his mom was killed, so he ended up not graduating with his class. But now he's going to Adult School, so it's not like he's a dropout, like his dad claims.

After the accident, Danny was in a daze. At first from shock, I guess. Then he started smoking pot, which he'd never done before. At least I don't think he had. And he was drinking, too. A lot. That went on for months. But now he almost never drinks more than a beer or two anymore, and I think he's totally quit smoking weed. Because of me, he says. Because I'm there for him.

Kneeling down in my closet I reach way into the back, to the slippers I never use anymore because they're too small for me. Feeling around in the toe of the right slipper, I pull out a foil packet that contains a condom. From the left slipper I take a can of foam. I put the can and the foil package under my pillow. We *never* do that stupid unprotected sex thing. From the very beginning we've known we wouldn't want a baby for a very long time. And I didn't want anything messing with my hormones, like the pill would. "That's cool," Danny'd said. "We're in this together."

I get soap from the bathroom and rub it along the window frame, opening and closing the window to be sure it will work easily, silently, when Danny gets here. What time will my mom turn out the light in her bedroom, I wonder. Is Danny already standing in the dark, back by the garage, waiting for all the lights but mine to go off?

It seems so juvenile, to be sneaking around to have sex. I'm practically an adult—in February I'll be old enough to vote. Why should I have to sneak around? On the other hand, it's not like I've ever said to my mom, "Hey Mom, do you mind if Danny comes over for sex tonight? We promise not to make too much noise." What would she say? She'd totally flip, I know.

She's sort of a modern mom, I guess. Even before I got my first period she'd talked to me about babies, and birth control, and protection from sexually transmitted diseases. But I still think she'd go nuts if she knew Danny sometimes comes over late at night, and we have sex in my room. I'll bet if one of her friends at work asked her if I was a virgin, she'd say probably not. She's not stupid. But I can't imagine coming right out and talking to her about how Danny and I are with each other. How would I start? "Hey, Mom, guess what Danny and I did last night in my room?" I don't think so.

I try to get back into biology again, but it's no use. I can't think about anything but Danny, and his dad, and I keep wondering why Danny had to leave and go to Alex's anyway. I know he gets really upset when his dad is on his case, but couldn't he have just gone into his room and turned up the stereo or something?

I set the alarm for five in the morning, hoping I can study better tomorrow. Two hours would do it. I leave the clock on my desk, where I'll have to get out of bed to turn it off. If I put it beside my bed I'd probably turn it off without even waking up. My plan is to study until seven, then shower and grab a piece of toast, and be ready for the biology test.

On my desk, next to the clock and in front of the picture of me and Danny at last year's Winter Fantasy, is a stack of college applications. I'm applying to six different schools, but the one I want is the University of California at Davis. They've got a great school of animal husbandry. Even though my grades and SAT scores are good, and I've got all of that Humane Society experience, I still may not get in. Davis is amazingly competitive. That's why I'm applying at other schools, too. For back up.

I pick up the Winter Fantasy picture and look carefully into

Danny's face. He's smiling a big, happy smile, showing his straight white teeth and the deep dimple in his cheek. He's wearing a tux, with a red bow tie. I'm in a white satin dress that I borrowed from April and, although I'd never say this out loud to anyone because it sounds so conceited, Danny and I looked really good together that night. I hope someday again I'll see him looking as happy as he does in the picture.

About ten minutes after my mom's light goes out, there's a gentle tapping at my window. I hold Kitty's mouth shut.

"Quiet," I say.

I let go of her mouth. Just as she's about to bark I clamp my hand around her muzzle again.

"Quiet!"

She gets the idea and lies down, watching me. I turn off my lamp, then raise my window and unhook the screen. Danny climbs through so quietly I can barely hear him myself, and I'm standing right next to him. He puts his arms around me and kisses me, hard.

The light from the street lamp in front of our house reflects softly through my open window. My eyes slowly adjust to the near darkness. I trace the outline of Danny's face with my fingers—his already slightly wrinkled forehead, his small straight nose, the little scar on his lower jaw, the outline of his lips.

I lean my face into his jacket and pull quickly away. It reeks.

"What?" he says, frowning.

"You quit smoking that stuff?"

"Oh," he says, his face relaxing into a grin. "Alex brought me over and we waited in his car until after the lights went out. He and Scott were smoking out—not me—no more bud for me. I told you."

He takes off his jacket and drops it out the still open window, laughing softly.

"It can air out down there. I'll pick it up on the way out."

He kisses me again, gently this time.

"We don't want to stink up your room with that stuff," he says. "What would your mom think about that?"

We both laugh, quietly, then sit down, side by side on the bed, arms touching. Danny leans his head on my shoulder.

"Speaking of parents," I say, "your dad called here tonight."

"Why?" Danny asks, sitting up straight and turning to face me.

"Looking for you. He sounded angry."

"He's always angry," Danny says. "I've got to get out of there, get my own place."

"Could you pay for it?"

"I'll have to figure something out."

"I saw some Help Wanted signs at the mall the other day."

"Yeah, well . . . let's not talk about that stuff right now," he says, pulling me toward him and kissing me on the lips. I get a taste of breath mint and wonder if Danny's being super considerate or if he has something to hide. Since I've been trying to get him to cut back on his drinking he covers things up sometimes.

I push back a bit. "Won't you have to get a job if you want your own place?"

Danny sighs. "Now you're sounding like my dad. *He's* always telling me get a job. I thought you were on *my* side."

"I *am* on your side. I'm always on your side," I tell him, pulling him to me, kissing him. We sit on my bed, close, holding hands and sometimes kissing, little light kisses on the lips and cheeks and forehead, not saying much for awhile. Danny runs his hand gently through my hair, following strands that reach to the middle of my back. Then he lies back and pulls me down beside him. We kiss, tongues touching. My breathing quickens, matching Danny's. We fumble at each other's clothes. Danny strips off his shirt and pants. I pull my T-shirt over my head and feel his hands unfasten my bra.

The light from the hallway comes on, spreading under the crack of my closed door. Danny jumps up and into the closet, pulling the door quickly, quietly, closed behind him. I scramble under the covers, pulling the blanket over our newly removed shirts, then lie still, listening, hoping Rocky doesn't decide to come crawl in bed with me as she sometimes does if she wakes up scared. Finally, I hear the toilet flush. The light goes out, and I know Rocky is back in her own room. I wait to be sure, then get up and open the closet door.

Danny and I ease silently back into my bed. He leans on one elbow, looking down at my face, taking my hand and guiding it to him, to where he wants to be touched. I strain upward to reach his lips with mine. The rhythms of our breathing match, faster. Hearts pounding, faster. Danny reaches under my pillow and removes the foil-wrapped packet. He carefully rolls on the condom, while I insert foam. An instant, only an instant, and then we are locked together.

After it's over Danny cries, heaving short sobs that pass in moments. With his head on my chest, my arms wrapped tightly around him, his tears wet against my skin, we sleep for awhile. Then, long before daylight, Danny gets up and dresses, kisses me on the forehead, and climbs back out my window, into the night.

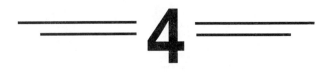

"It's seven-thirty," Mom says, shaking me gently.

"Seven-thirty?" I bolt out of bed, suddenly awake. "What happened to my alarm clock?"

Mom picks up the clock from my desk. "You must have slept through it."

"Oh, man," I say, thinking about all the biology I didn't study.

During English, first period, I try to review my biology notes, but Ms. Lee keeps calling on me to answer questions about *Macbeth*. The part I most relate to at this moment is the witch's—"Double, double, toil and trouble/Fire burn and cauldron bubble."

Double trouble is what I find in biology. I make all kinds of guesses, about something called reverse transcriptase, and somatic mutations, but as far as the biology test goes, I could be the poster child for "Clueless Syndrome."

At lunch April and I go over to Barb and Edie's. April orders one of their famous garbageburgers. I get a grilled cheese sandwich. Ever since I started working at the Humane Society, I lost my taste for dead animals.

"I'm *starving*," April says as we wait for our order to come up. "I couldn't even eat last night I got so nervous about driving."

"How'd it go?" I ask.

"Fine. I only nearly killed us three times. I think my dad's seeing his doctor today for tranquilizers."

"It couldn't have been *that* bad. Weren't you driving at the race track parking lot? There're never any cars there at night."

"Who said anything about cars? There're posts, and fences, and a couple of trees, plus eight admission gates. All kinds of stuff just jumps out at you over there."

April cracks me up. She's been trying to learn to drive since she got her learner's permit at fifteen. She *still* doesn't have her license and she'll be eighteen soon. In April, of course. I'm glad my parents didn't name *me* after my birth month. I can hear it now, February Arredondo. What a mouthful *that* would be. Erica Joan Arredondo's bad enough. The Joan is after my mom's mom. I don't love the name, but I love my gramma, so that makes the name sound better to me.

Sometimes I fantasize that Erica Lara would be better, but that's a long way away. I've got other things to worry about right now. Like I'm pretty sure I failed my biology test.

"Hey, aren't you going to finish your lunch?" April says.

I hear hunger in her voice, even though she's just practically inhaled a whole garbageburger and a large, meaning huge, order of fries.

"You can have it. I'm not so hungry."

"What's wrong?" she asks, reaching for my sandwich and taking a bite in one quick move. April eats a lot for a skinny girl.

"I'm just not very hungry," I say.

"Are things okay with Dan the man?"

"Great," I say, remembering last night, how he held me tight and told me he would always love me, nothing could ever change that.

"Well? There's a reason a healthy, red-blooded girl like yourself loses her appetite. Pregnant?"

"April!" I say, tossing my wadded-up napkin at her. "Get a grip on your imagination, will you?"

"Oh, yeah. Like it never happens."

"It's not happening to me," I say. "That's just stupid."

"You ought to become a born-again virgin," April says. "I'm glad I did—celibate for a year now and worry free—no pregnancy worries, no STD worries—like that poor Sandra with AIDS."

"I don't have to worry about that, either," I say. "We're really careful."

"Not only pregnancy and disease stuff. I used to worry all the time about my mom and dad freaking out if they found out I was doing the big *IT*."

"April, if we're old enough to choose the President of the United States, don't you think we're old enough to make our own decisions about sex?" I say.

"I suppose your parents are totally aware and supportive of the sexual activities in which you and Danny are engaged?" April asks, holding a spoon in front of my face, as if it's a microphone.

I push it away. "I'm not your talk show guest," I remind her, laughing.

"Be honest, though. Wouldn't your parents orbit the solar system if they knew for sure their little girl was involved in an affair of passion?"

"Honestly, I'm not sure," I say, remembering how scared I felt last night when Rocky got up to go to the bathroom. We were lucky the little spy went back to her own room. But what if we'd been discovered? We're not doing anything wrong, are we—just loving each other?

"Something's taking your mind off eating," April says, grabbing the other half of my sandwich.

"The biology test last period—I messed up big time," I say, as we dump our trash and walk back toward Hamilton High.

"You always think you mess up on tests, and you always end up with a big fat *A*, so I don't want to hear it."

"This time is different," I say.

"Yeah, yeah, yeah. You're breaking my heart. If I miss one more government assignment I won't even graduate."

"Don't *miss* another government assignment," I tell her.

"But it's boring," April says.

"Sometimes we've got to do boring stuff," I say, and then I feel like washing my mouth out with soap. I hate when I sound like my mom. If I'm not careful, pretty soon I'll be like "you only get out of it what you put into it." Or, "when life gives you lemons, make lemonade."

"Do you want to go to the mall with me and Morgan?" April says.

"I can't. I've got to study for the biology make-up. And calculus, too."

April makes a face at me. "You worry too much. Lighten up."

"I really want to be accepted to UC Davis in animal husbandry," I remind her.

"I'm glad I have low aspirations," April says, putting the last bite of my grilled cheese sandwich in her mouth.

On the way back to school April starts quoting talk show hosts.

"Seventy-six percent of the girls in this survey said teenagers have sex because the boy wants it, not the girl. And most girls regret it later."

"Well, that leaves 24 percent with a different opinion," I say.

"Don't go getting mathematical on me."

"You're the one who started it with your talk show statistics."

"No, but don't you think that's true? Most girls just do it to please the guys?" April says.

We pause at the hallway, where we have to go in separate directions to our lockers.

"I don't know about most girls," I say.

"I think I just wanted to make Wade happy. It wasn't for me."

The first bell rings and we rush toward our lockers.

"See you in Peer Counseling," April says.

I make my way past crowds of kids to try to get to my locker, which is in the middle of where the Asian kids hang out—Chinese, Vietnamese, Cambodian, Korean, Japanese, Thai—I can't exactly tell the difference, I just know there is one. Like with me, everyone assumes because of my name and the way I look that I'm Mexican, but really, my dad's family is from Columbia and my mom is a mix of a lot of things. Her mother is from Mexico, but my grampa's only half Mexican and the other half German.

One of the good things about Hamilton High is that most of the people here, students *and* teachers, judge you for who you are and not for your name or the color of your skin.

When I was younger and still going to school overseas where my dad was stationed, a lot of the officers' kids were white and sometimes they'd tease me—call me names like Erica Hairy Donut instead of Erica Arredondo, or once, when someone I thought was my friend got mad at me, she called me a dirty Mexican. I hate that stuff.

My mom told me just to forget it. The little girl was ignorant and I should feel sorry for her. I couldn't forget it, though, and we were never really friends again. But Hamilton High has practically every kind of person you can imagine here, so no one really stands out as weird.

I dump my books in my locker, except for my notebook, and go to class. I sit in the back, next to April. Brett sits down on the other side of April and whispers something to her, "Don't tell anyone about my cousin. Okay?"

"Don't worry," April says, flashing me a look that says "Keep your mouth shut."

We have outside speakers two or three times a month in this class, and they're usually really interesting. There was a group from the Gay and Lesbian Rights League last week, and a woman running for Congress the week before. We've had people from Alcoholics Anonymous, and a Jewish woman who survived Auschwitz.

God. It's one thing to know about Anne Frank, and to learn the historical facts of millions of concentration camp deaths, and it's another to hear stories, face to face, from someone who's been through it all.

"AIDS again?" Colin says, reading the agenda on the chalkboard. He dumps his books on the desk in front of me and sits down.

"Don't you think enough is enough?" he asks. "AIDS prevention assemblies, AIDS awareness week in biology, AIDS talks in P.E. We get it, we get it."

"We want to be sure," Woodsy says, walking past us to greet the speakers.

Colin blushes and puts his head down on the desk. He's got red hair and light, light skin, so it's really obvious when he gets embarrassed, which is a lot of the time.

Ms. Woods, Woodsy, introduces the four speakers from the AIDS Center, two men and two women. They each take turns telling their stories. It is unbelievably sad. One of the women, Alma, didn't even know she was HIV positive until she was seven months pregnant. Her little girl, who is now five, has full-blown AIDS. The mother still doesn't even have any symptoms.

When I read in the newspaper about babies with AIDS, I always think the moms must be sluts and addicts who don't care about anyone or anything. The moms deserve everything they get, but their innocent little babies shouldn't have to pay.

It makes me think. Alma's one of the moms I would hate if I read about her in the paper, but to meet her and to hear her story, I see that she's doing everything she possibly can for her daughter. And the way she got the virus was from her *husband*, who she never even suspected was running around with prostitutes, women *and* men, until she got the surprise results of a blood test.

"You have to take care of yourselves," she tells us. "Assume whoever you might be involved with carries the disease, and act accordingly."

"But my boyfriend and I have been together for two years," Darlene says. "We've never even been with anyone else."

"My husband and I had been together for ten years," Alma says. "I didn't think he was with anyone else, either. Do you think your boyfriend would tell you if he got drunk at a party and had sex with someone he hardly even knew? Do you think that never happens?"

"Not with *my* boyfriend," Darlene says.

"I hope not," Alma says. "Of course there are people who are committed to one another and never stray. I thought I was in a marriage like that. You think you're in a relationship like that. I was wrong, but I hope you're right."

One of the men, Sam, is very tough looking—all buffed out, with tattoos on both arms. He talks about his former drug use, how it completely robbed him of his family and ten years of his life, and now that he's clean, it's still robbing him of life, because he's HIV positive and beginning to see symptoms of AIDS. He demonstrates how to sterilize needles, pleading with us not to use drugs, but saying that if we *are* involved with drugs we should at least take precautions against disease.

"How can anyone do that to themselves?" April asks when Sam brings out the long hypodermic needle.

I think of how my gramma has to give herself an injection of insulin every day. "I guess people get used to it if they do it often enough," I say.

After school I'm waiting at the bus stop, reading my English assignment. It's this really weird story about a guy who wakes up in the morning to find he's turned into a giant beetle overnight. Unbelievable. I don't know where Ms. Lee comes up with this stuff. It's by a famous writer, someone named Kafka, but it's weird anyway.

"Hey, Pups!"

I look up from the story to see Danny leaning out the window of Alex's old beat-up Honda Civic.

"Want a ride?"

"Sure."

I jump in the back seat, then lean forward and give Danny a quick kiss on the cheek.

"Hi, Erica," Alex says. His skinny arm is resting lightly on the edge of the open window, his scraggly blond hair hanging over the back of the seat. He still doesn't look like much, but I like Alex better than I did the first time I met him at the Humane Society. I thought he was a total jerk that day. Now that I've gotten to know him, he only seems like a jerk about half the time.

"Thanks for giving me a ride," I say. "The bus takes forever."

"No problem," Alex says, turning and flashing a quick smile at me.

"We have to make one fast stop on the way, then we'll drop you at your house," Danny says.

"I'm kind of in a hurry," I tell Danny. "I didn't get much studying done last night," I say with a sly smile.

"You had better things to do," he smiles back.

"We heard this really sad story in Peer Counseling today," I tell Danny and Alex. "This woman who didn't even know she was HIV positive . . ."

"I've got enough on my mind. Don't tell me any sad stories," Danny says, before I even get to the part about the baby.

Alex pulls up in front of Danny's house.

"This'll only take a minute," Danny says. "C'mon, you can help carry stuff."

I follow them to the front door. Danny takes out his key and turns it in the lock, but he can't get the door open.

"He's got that special inside lock on," Danny says. "Let's go to the back."

"Look at your mom's garden," Alex says, indicating a weed-filled section of the yard that used to be a flower bed.

I didn't know Danny's mom long, Irene, her name was, but she loved flowers.

"She's turning over in her grave, man," Alex says. "We should come clear this out and plant stuff."

Danny stands looking at the space where tulips and hollyhocks grew last spring. I stand next to him, holding his hand.

"Shit," he says, then turns and walks away.

When we get to the back door, there's a shiny new padlock securing it.

"Bastard," Danny says. "He's locked me out of my own place!"

"Why?" I ask.

Alex goes back to his car for a screwdriver.

"I don't know. He got all pissed when he called Adult School yesterday and found out that I haven't been attending."

"You haven't?" I ask, surprised.

"Oh, God, Pups. It's just so boring."

"That's why he locked you out?"

"He tried to ground me because I'm not working and I'm not going to school. That's not even legal! He can't ground an adult."

"Hey," Alex calls, waving a very long screwdriver.

Together, Danny and Alex try to get the window open that leads to Danny's bedroom. When that doesn't work, they try all of the other windows. Finally they go back to Danny's window. Danny takes the handle of the screwdriver and breaks the window, near the lock. He taps glass away, making an opening big enough for his hand, then reaches through, unlocks the window, and opens it. With a rag from the car they wipe the broken glass shards off the sill.

"I'll climb through," Danny says. "I've had practice." He gives me a big smile, then climbs through the window.

"Here," he says, starting to hand stuff out.

Alex opens the Honda's hatchback and we carry books and tapes, shirts, pants, underwear, shoes, a tennis racquet, a soccer ball, all kinds of stuff. It seems like there's not room for one more thing when Danny hands out first one stereo speaker and then another. Alex laughs.

"You think he's pissed now, wait 'til he finds this missing."

"Shit. He never listens to music anyway. Besides, the speakers at your house are shot."

Danny has one foot over the window sill, climbing out, when two police cars pull into the driveway. Three policemen jump from the second car and crouch behind it, guns drawn.

"Put your hands over your heads," a voice from a bullhorn demands.

"Fuck!" Alex says, raising his hands.

I'm shaking so bad I can barely put my hands up, but somehow I manage. Danny starts to get out of the window.

"FREEZE! Hands up," the voice yells.

Danny sits on the sill, his hands up.

"I live here," Danny yells.

"Sure you do," the voice says, all sarcastic.

5

"**I** can't tell you how frightening it is to be summoned from a meeting for an emergency call from the police department!"

We are sitting in the kitchen, at the oak table, Rocky's eyes wide with the experience of having been to the police station and seen her sister released from behind closed doors, like a criminal out on bail in a TV play.

"I thought you or Rochelle had been in some horrible accident, or kidnapped, or Gramma'd been found dead . . . "

"I'm sorry, Mom. It wasn't my fault!"

"You chose to help Danny and Alex break into a house. Whose fault was that?"

"Mom, it wasn't just any house. It was *Danny's* house."

"No. It is *not* Danny's house. It's Danny's father's house."

"Well, Danny's father locked him out. Alex's mom said he could stay there, so he just went home to get his things. That's all."

"Did you see a murderer when you were in jail?" Rocky asks.

"This is not a joke, Rochelle!" Mom says.

"I'm not joking," Rochelle says.

"If those Neighborhood Watch people would mind their own business . . ."

"Erica! It is not the fault of Neighborhood Watch, or Danny's father, or the police! What you were doing was wrong!"

We're silent long enough that Rocky gets bored and goes outside to play with Kitty.

"I don't know what to think," Mom says. "You've always had so much common sense, but where Danny's concerned, good sense takes a vacation."

"But Mom . . . "

"Really, if Danny had taken you to kill his father, rather than just rob from him, would you have gone along with it?"

"Mom! Danny took his own stuff!"

"What about the stereo speakers?"

"His dad doesn't even listen to the stereo," I say, knowing as soon as I've said it how lame it sounds.

I pick up my books and go back to my bedroom, leaving Mom sitting at the table. I wonder if Danny and Alex are out yet. It was different for me because I'm only seventeen. A policewoman took me to the station and had me sit in the waiting room until my mom came. But Alex and Danny are considered adults. They were handcuffed and everything.

As soon as Danny's dad is notified of the situation, he should be able to clear everything up—if he wants to. But what if he decides to press charges?

When I first got acquainted with Danny's dad, he seemed like an ordinary dad, kind of quiet, but pleasant enough. It was fun to go to their house. Irene always had some project going, and as soon as anyone walked in the door she'd yell at them to come help her. Cooking, planting flowers, refinishing furniture, quilting, always something.

Even if Mr. Lara didn't always seem interested, he was never mean. I guess maybe he misses her as much as Danny does and they take it out on each other. I wish they could help each other out instead of making things worse. At least I hope Mr. Lara will help Danny and Alex get released from custody.

"Erica?" Mom calls softly at my closed bedroom door.

I open it, careful to avoid eye contact.

"Why don't you come have a bowl of soup with me and Rocky?

You must be hungry."

I walk out to the kitchen and sit down at the table. Mom hands me a bowl of chicken soup, left over from last night, and puts toasted bagels and carrot sticks on the table.

"I guess this will hold us until tomorrow. Something got in the way of my plan to go to the market after work," Mom says with a sigh.

Things start closing in on me, my mom's sadness, the look of curiosity and confusion on Rochelle's face as she sneaks glimpses of me over her soup bowl, the anxiety over not knowing what's happening with Danny and Alex at the police station.

"Give me your list, Mom. I'll go to the market for you," I say.

She gives me a long look. "No, I don't think I want you out driving around tonight."

I feel such a distance between us. My whole life my mom's trusted me, and now she looks at me like I'm a stranger, and acts as if I can't be trusted to go to the market.

"Whatever," I say, and go back to my room to study.

Between outlining the biology chapter, section by section, and writing out note cards, and visualizing each process as it's explained, I begin to understand a bit about prokaryotes and viruses. But all the time I'm working on biology, I'm also worrying about Danny. Images of police brutality crowd out pictures of microfossils and I imagine Danny and Alex, on the floor of a cell, being brutally beaten—like I saw Rodney King being beaten on video tape in my social issues class.

I call Alex's number but there's no answer. Then I call Danny's house, but there's no answer there, either. I even call the police station and ask if Danny Lara and Alex Kendall are still being held. They don't give out any information. I knew that, but I had to try, anyway.

I set biology aside and open my literature textbook, finding where I left off in "Metamorphosis." Poor Gregor Samsa, even though he's turned into a beetle, his main worry is his job. That's all his parents seem to care about, too, just that he can keep supporting them. His sister's the only one who seems to really care about

Gregor but even she's so disgusted she can't look at him.

Gregor is in a kind of jail, too, where he can't leave his room because he's too frightening a sight to other people. He's hurt, and no one even knows to help him. God. I hope Danny's not hurt. I feel so helpless, just sitting here, waiting.

Finally, around nine, the phone rings and it's Danny.

"What happened?" I ask him.

"Alex's mom got us released to her custody. My dad wouldn't even bother to come to the station."

"Did you call him?"

"Yeah, my one phone call. What a waste. He told me I got myself into the mess, I could just get myself out."

Is it my imagination, or are Danny's words kind of slurry?

"I'm a big boy now, my dad said. Then he started yelling at me about how I had to pay for the broken window—it's got to be fixed right now 'cause he's getting ready to sell the house. He *told* me that, while I was being held by the cops!"

"He's selling your house?"

"Yeah. The house I grew up in, that the three of us fixed up all together. I'll probably never, ever, even be inside that house again."

There's a long pause and I think Danny is struggling for control.

"And then he started in on how the stereo speakers got messed up when I disconnected them. 'Thanks for your help, Dad,' I told him, and then I hung up while he was still blab-blabbing away."

"What did Alex's mom say?"

"She's cool. Getting us out tonight was nothing compared to what Joey put her through. The cops all still remember her from when they were picking Joey up all the time."

"Was she mad?"

"No. She was a little, you know, feeling no pain."

"From drinking? And they released you to her?"

"Yeah. They don't give a shit. They'd of had to release us pretty soon, anyway."

I start to tell Danny how upset my mom is.

"My wrists are all bruised, where they slapped the cuffs on me."

"I was so worried they'd hurt you."

"Pigs. They fucked up Alex's arm when they shoved him in the car. If we'd been some of those little Sycamore Hills rich boys they'd have been gentle, but with us? Shoving guys like us around is how they get their nuts off."

I'm pretty sure from the way he's talking that Danny's been drinking.

"My mom is *so* mad at me . . . "

"My dad's a number one asshole."

Yep. For sure he's been drinking.

I try one more time to tell Danny about the argument with my mom, but he interrupts with "Alex has to call Gina now, Pups. We'll talk later. Maybe I'll stop by after everything's quiet."

"Not tonight," I tell him. "Things are too weird around here."

"Maybe tomorrow night," he says. He hangs up without tapping three times.

I know Mom being mad at me is not as big a thing as being handcuffed and shoved around by the police, but I wish Danny would have had time to listen. I remember that time in Alex's car, too, when I was trying to tell Danny about the woman with AIDS, and he didn't want to hear any sad stories. I wonder why we always have time for his stories, but never for mine. Well, "always/never." That *is* an exaggeration. Besides, my troubles really aren't as big as Danny's—no mom, and a dad who doesn't care. No wonder he's having a hard time.

I dial April's number, knowing she'll listen, but she's not home.

About ten-thirty, after Rocky's asleep, Mom comes in and sits at the end of my bed, across from the desk where I'm still reading. She's in her purple robe. Her face is clean and shiny from moisturizer, but her beginning frown wrinkles are deeper than usual.

"I want to talk to you," she says.

I *don't* want to talk, but I'm sure there's no way to get out of it.

"I'm so worried about you, Erica. I don't think you're taking school as seriously as you always have, and I think you're letting Danny run your life."

"That's not true! I care about Danny. I *love* Danny. But he doesn't run my life."

"Anyone who can get you to assist them in a robbery has too much influence over you. You are not a thief, Erica. I know that business today wasn't your idea."

"That was hardly a *robbery*, Mom. You're making things lots worse than they really are."

"I'm making things worse? *I'm* not the one who was *arrested*!"

I sit petting Kitty, not knowing what to say.

"Your biology teacher called me at work this afternoon," Mom says. "I go along for years, hearing only good things about you and then on this one day I get two phone calls, first from the school and then from the police department. What's happening, Erica? Is it drugs?"

"Drugs? Is that what you think?"

"I don't know what to think. All of those 'is your child on drugs' check lists talk about sudden shifts in behavior and attitude."

"Well, I don't do drugs, Mom. I'm not stupid."

"And I'm not stupid, either. I know all kinds of things go on at Alex's house, and I know you hang out there sometimes, because Alice at work told me she saw our car there."

"I don't *hang out* there, Mom. I've probably been there about three times in my whole life, and that's just been to drop Danny off, or pick him up or something like that."

"Well, I want you to stay away from there. According to Alice it's like a magnet for low lifes."

I think back to the lecture I got from the policewoman at the station this afternoon. She'd said I look like too nice a person to be hanging out with the likes of Danny and Alex. "Lie down with dogs, get up with fleas," she'd told me. I told her I work at the Humane Society and I like dogs. She said she did, too, but not the human kind.

"I think Danny's made a very bad choice, to move in with Alex. I just hope you're not making bad choices right along with him."

I sigh. "Mom, are you mad at me because of some rumor you've heard about the place Alex lives?"

Mom gives me a long look, then says, more calmly. "You're right. That's not fair . . . Mrs. Costanza says she's concerned about you—your last two tests have not been good, and your homework's not up to its usual standards."

I shake my head in disbelief. April's barely getting *D*s in some of her classes and no one ever calls her parents. I let my grade in biology drop to a *B* plus and the communications systems are buzzing.

"Erica . . . " Mom takes a deep breath. "Are you pregnant?"

I turn around in my chair to look my mother straight in the eyes. I'm so angry I can feel the rhythm of my heart pounding in my head.

"You accuse me of being a thief! You think I'm on drugs! You think I'm pregnant! I make one simple mistake of being in the wrong place at the wrong time and all of a sudden you think the worst of me!"

"I don't think the worst of you. I just don't know what to think!"

We are both crying now. Mom's face is red and mine must be, too. Kitty is whimpering at my feet, looking back and forth between me and Mom.

"You never tell me anything anymore," Mom says, "and when I ask you anything personal you always avoid the question . . ."

Always, never, I think. I take a deep breath and try to calm down, to remember what I've learned in Peer Counseling, about communication patterns.

"We're both really upset, Mom. Could we sleep on all of this and talk some more in the morning?"

It turns out my mom didn't take that class.

"I'm not finished," she says, angrily. "I know you care about Danny. But he's going nowhere with his life, and if you stay with him he'll drag you down too. You'd be better off without him."

"Mom . . . you wouldn't say that if you knew Danny the way I do."

"I know what I see, Erica, and I see you not doing as well in school, and getting arrested, and I see Danny not working . . ."

"He's *planning* to get a job . . ."

". . . not finishing school, just floating along. I don't respect that. I just don't think he's right for you."

"I'm the only one who can judge who's right for me," I say. "I love Danny, and he loves me."

"I want you to broaden your scope a bit, start dating other boys."

"But that's not what *I* want! You're treating me like I'm Rochelle's age."

Kitty lumbers over to Mom and lays her head on Mom's leg. Mom scratches Kitty behind the ears, then sighs.

"You've done so well all through high school, and you've always been such a delight as a daughter, I just don't want anything to go wrong for you at this stage of your life, and I'm afraid you're much too serious with Danny."

"But Mom, *I* have to decide what's right for me. I'll be on my own at college in less than a year. I'm not a child anymore. Look at you. You were *married* when you were my age."

"Yes, well sometimes I wish I'd listened to *my* mother about that."

"Gramma *loves* Dad," I say.

"But she thought I was too young to get married, and in a way she was right. I'd have been better off if I'd gone to college."

"And not have been bothered with Dad, or me, or Rochelle?" I ask, ready to be even more angry at her answer.

"It's not that simple, Erica. You know I love Dad. And I can't imagine not being your mom, or Rochelle's mom. It's just that I don't want you to do *anything* that will get in the way of going to college and becoming a veterinarian. I want you to be smarter than I was."

"I'm *going* to college, and I'm going to be a vet. You don't have to worry about that. But you can't tell me not to see Danny."

"Would you at least go out with other boys now and then?"

"Maybe," I say, knowing I won't do that, but tired of the argument.

Mom sighs. "Well, I guess I can remember what it's like to be seventeen and in love. But that was different."

"Why?"

"Dad was a responsible person, working, going to school. Your dad was never lazy, and he never blamed anyone else for his problems. Danny's life seems to be getting worse and worse, and it's never his fault."

"You just don't know him the way I do," I say.

"Sometimes I wonder if you know Danny as well as you think you do."

Late in the night, when it's early in the morning in Germany, I hear Mom talking to the overseas operator, trying to get through to

Dad. Because I know she'll be talking about me, I open my door a crack to listen.

I catch bits and pieces of what my mom is saying—arrested, Danny, school.

"I talked to her about seeing other boys . . . I think maybe she will."

There's a long silence from Mom, so I guess Dad is giving her his ideas on the whole subject. Then Mom says, "I'm so tired of trying to be mother and father both to these girls. Rochelle's always been a handful, but I didn't expect such problems with Erica."

Whatever Dad says back to Mom makes her mad.

"That's easy for you to say, isn't it? You'll come waltzing in here at Christmastime, the returning hero, while I've been doing all of the everyday dirty work for the past five years."

I get up and close the door. I can't wait to go away to college and live my own life. At least that will be one less kid for my mom to complain about.

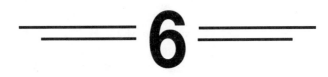
It is one of those "I'm glad to be alive" days in the San Gabriel Valley. A brisk wind has blown away the smog, leaving clear blue skies and fluffy white clouds. From where I'm standing, on the second floor of the Humane Society, near the volunteers' office, I can see the Whittier Hills to my left, and south, and a bit of the Los Angeles skyline is off to my right. Directly below are the animal cages, with vine-covered lattice work offering shade for each pen.

Sinclair comes out of the office and leans on the railing next to me.

"Taking a break?"

"I was dying of thirst," I say, offering him a swallow of my soda.

"No thanks . . . What a day, huh?"

"I wish they could all be like this."

"Not me. I *love* variety," he says.

"Even smog?"

"Well, that helps us appreciate days like this."

"Are you always up, Sinclair?"

"Almost always," Sinclair says. "We're surrounded by so much beauty, why dwell on the ugly—that's my philosophy."

We hear several soft gurgling coos from the doves in the atrium behind us. Sinclair laughs. "They like my philosophy," he says.

"How's Daniel? You still together?"

"A year December 17," I say.

"Not bad for kids," he smiles.

I turn to look at him. His gentle eyes and soft smile invite conversation.

"My mom thinks I shouldn't see Danny anymore," I say. Then I tell Sinclair all about getting arrested, and how Danny's stopped going to school, and how he's moved in with Alex and Alex's mom.

"Alex is a strange one," Sinclair says. "He can be so cold and hard with people, but he was good with the animals the few times he volunteered here."

"I know. Sometimes I like Alex a lot, and sometimes I think he's the biggest jerk in the world."

Just then one of the animal control officers, Antoinette, comes in through the back gate, carrying a medium-sized black and white dog. It looks like the dog is sick, and Antoinette looks very angry. I walk downstairs to see what's happening and Sinclair follows close behind. Antoinette goes directly to the infirmary and places the dog, gently, on a padded mat in a clean cage. She dips her hand in the water dish and lets the dog lick her fingers. The dog can barely hold its head up.

"I don't know if we'll save this one or not, she's so dehydrated and malnourished," she says. "People piss me off so bad!"

The dog is so skinny every rib shows and even the contours of her skull are exaggerated. Her black coat is dull and matted, she's flea-ridden, and she has big bald patches of scabby skin all over her back.

"According to the neighbors, the dog's owners are out of town a lot," Antoinette says, angrily.

Sinclair reaches in and gently lifts the dog's chin, so he can see her eyes. "Poor baby," he says.

"Erica, go get a puppy mixture for her, would you? Only about half a serving. We've got to start her slow. I'll dust her with flea powder. And just look at that mange. Jesus!"

I wouldn't want to be the owner of this dog and run into Antoinette anywhere. Antoinette is tall and solid and she's an amateur volleyball player. She's strong, and I've seen so much anger in her eyes when she brings in a mistreated animal that she scares *me*, and I would never (this time never is the right word), *never* mistreat an animal.

When I bring the food back I give the dog a few bites, just to give her a taste, and then set the bowl right next to her. She looks up at me without moving her head and gives her tail a barely perceptible wag.

"So listen, girl," Sinclair says as we walk back to the office. "I desperately need help on this mobile pet adoption thing I'm doing at the library tonight, and all but one of my volunteers have flaked out on me."

I think of all the homework I have waiting for me. But things are still really awkward between me and my mom, so I'm in no hurry to go home.

"Will you go? Just until nine?"

"Sure," I say.

I call Mom and tell her she doesn't have to pick me up from work, that I'll be doing the mobile adoption thing at the library, then I go brush the dogs that are scheduled for the mobile unit.

"You look so handsome, someone's sure to fall in love with you tonight," I tell the black lab as I brush his back and chest.

Sinclair and I, and Beth, the fourteen-year-old volunteer who *didn't* flake out, check the van to be sure we've got poop bags and adoption forms, and posters and other publicity materials. As we walk back toward the kennels to get the dogs, the caracara throws back its head and lets loose with its warbling screech.

"Hel-*lo*!" Sinclair says, stopping to look at the bird. "Wanting some attention are you, you beautifully costumed and coiffed birdy?"

The bird makes a quick turn of the head, as if posing to give Sinclair a better view. Sinclair laughs.

"Don't you just *love* how the boys get to be the ones to dress up in the animal kingdom?"

"You dress up more than I do," Beth says.

"Choices, darlin'. I don't choose drab."

We get the dogs, four of them, and put them in the small cages in the van.

"It's only for a little while," Beth tells the black lab, who sticks his nose as far as it will go through a small section of the heavy wire cage. "And you, big baby, just calm down," she says, laughing at the brown dog who keeps turning in tight circles inside the cage.

Beth is really fat, and when I see her at school she's always looking down at the ground, walking with her books clutched in front of her. But with the animals she's totally different, laughing and talking, and when she walks along the corridors of the Humane Society, she looks straight ahead, not down.

"**L**ook, Mom, there's Eddie, from 'Frasier'! I want that one."
A girl about Rochelle's age comes running up to the brown terrier where I'm walking him, near the entrance of the library.

"Easy," I say, "Slow down so you don't scare him."

"I want this one," she says, leaning down to pet him.

"This is Jackie," I say. "He likes you."

Jackie is licking the girl's hands, face, legs, any exposed skin he can find.

"My mom said I could get a dog tonight, and this is the one I want. Here," she says, trying to take the leash from my hand.

"It's not that easy," I say, laughing.

The mom is over petting the black lab. "How about this one, Honey? I hear labs are really mellow."

Jackie is wrapping himself around the girl's legs, getting tangled in the leash.

"This one, Mom," the girl whines. "He's mellow, too."

The mom comes over to look at Jackie. "Don't you think the lab would be more of a family dog?" she asks.

"He's a wonderful dog," I say, watching the girl's expression turn from joy to uneasiness.

"But Jackie's wonderful, too—lots of energy and he's very affectionate."

"Will he chew things?"

"That's hard to predict. But we have free obedience training programs for our adopted pets. He's smart, so he'd probably be pretty easy to train."

"Can I take him, Mom?" the girl says, tugging on the leash again.

I explain that they have to fill out some adoption papers and then come to the Humane Society and talk with an adoption counselor before they can take the dog.

Just as I hand adoption forms to the mom and daughter, one of the librarians comes walking up to the van, carrying a cordless phone. She asks Sinclair, "Is there an Erica Arredondo with you?"

"I'm Erica," I say.

She hands me the phone and waits. It's Mom. "Oh, Erica? Shall I come get you about nine?"

"No thanks," I say. "Sinclair can drop me off."

"Sinclair?"

"You know. From the Humane Society."

"Oh. Good," she says, in one of those mom-curious tones that makes me think she's reading something weird into my ride home with Sinclair.

I hand the phone back to the librarian. I'd already told Mom I didn't need a ride. That was just an excuse to check up on me. It makes me feel strange, and sad, to think my mother doesn't trust me anymore.

During a quiet time I go into the library to look for an article about the guy who wrote "Metamorphosis." All of the books that have anything about Franz Kafka are already checked out. I guess Ms. Lee must have given the same assignment to all of her classes. I pick up the latest issue of *People* and take it over to one of the square tables in the reference section.

I sit at the dark, heavy wood table, the magazine open in front of me, absorbing the library atmosphere. The hushed conversations, the quiet air of books, the helpful, efficient librarians—it all feels so quietly safe. When we lived overseas, the base libraries were minimal, not like real libraries. The city libraries were often huge and beautiful, but the books were mostly in German, or Japanese, depending on where my dad was stationed. One of the first things I did when we moved to Hamilton Heights was to get my own library card.

I look out the window and see that nothing much is going on at the pet van, then I wander over to the travel section, near the entrance, and pick up a book about Germany. That's where my dad is right now. That's also the last place we lived, back when we all lived together on the base.

There's a picture of Linderhof Castle, where this weird guy, Prince Ludwig II, built his own version of Fantasyland long before

Walt Disney was ever around. And there are pictures of Augsburg, which is where we lived for awhile. It was like a whole different life, living in a town that was 2,000 years old and that was filled with buildings that were at least four or five hundred years old. In Hamilton Heights, the original Humane Society building is one of the oldest buildings still standing, and it's not even a hundred years old.

"Erica?"

I look up to see Beth. "Oh, sorry," I say, putting the book back on the shelf and catching up with her. She keeps her head down, eyes on the floor, as we walk past the busy check-out counter to the parking lot.

"I'm sorry, Sinclair. I guess I lost track of time."

"That happens to me in libraries, too," he says, smiling. "But help me get the dogs back in their cages now."

After the dogs are secure back in their own spaces, and we've emptied the poop bags, I wash and spray my shoes and go to check the black and white dog in the infirmary. She still hasn't eaten much. I hand-feed her a few bites.

"You'll be okay," I tell her. "You're someplace where people will love you and take care of you. But you've got to try."

Sinclair reaches in and touches her gently under the chin. "My poor, beautiful baby," he coos.

This dog is anything but beautiful, but Sinclair, as if he's read my mind, says, "If we see the beauty in her now, she'll soon be so beautiful everyone can see it."

"I just want her to start eating," I say.

We walk past the double green doors that lead to the forbidden section where drugs are kept and euthanasia performed. Beth is waiting for us by Sinclair's perfectly maintained old Dodge Dart. I climb in the back seat, leaving the front for Beth. Sinclair drops her off first, then takes me home. We sit in the driveway for a bit, talking.

"I can't believe it's only three weeks to Thanksgiving," Sinclair says.

"I know. I think my dad will be home by then."

"Do you have a big family Thanksgiving dinner?"

"We always do. Even when we were living overseas we usually managed the home for the holidays thing. How about you?"

"My family always does, but I'll probably just have a few friends in."

"Does your family live far away?"

"No. It's a long story, but, you know, my dad . . ."

I wait for Sinclair to finish his sentence, but he doesn't do it.

"My mom bakes a great pumpkin pie. She'll probably bring one over to me. But my dad . . . and my brothers . . . "

The kitchen door opens and Kitty comes bounding out. Sinclair opens his car door before she has a chance to jump up on it and scratch it. She jumps inside the car and sits up straight in the back seat, as if she's waiting for a chauffeur to take her somewhere. I get out and drag Kitty out, and Sinclair gets my books for me and carries them to the porch.

"Thanks for helping me out," he says. "I hate to cancel any event, and it's hard to manage with just two people, especially if one of them is too shy to talk."

"It was fun," I tell him. "And it looks as if at least two of the dogs have found a home."

"Yep, another success for the traveling zoo," he laughs.

Mom comes to the door and calls Kitty in, and I introduce her to Sinclair. They talk long enough to be polite, then Sinclair leaves and I take my books back to my bedroom desk. Mom follows, looking a bit haggard.

I'm sort of mad at her for calling the library to check up on me tonight, but it's not worth the trouble to confront her.

"Erica, I'm glad you've decided to see other people . . ."

"See other people?" I think, trying to figure out what Mom's talking about.

"And you know I'm not prejudiced. But I hope you'll think long and hard before you get involved with an African American."

I'm speechless.

"Not that he wouldn't be as good as anyone else. I don't mean that. But even though we've come a long way, social attitudes still make mixed relationships very difficult. Sue and Jack at work, both wonderful people, but it's hard . . ."

"*What* are you talking about, Mom?"

"Well, you seem really to like Sinclair . . ."

"Mom! I told you. I love Danny. He loves me."

"Well, but I just want to warn you, Erica. I don't want you to be hurt. And you and Sinclair seem fond of each other."

Suddenly, the tension of the last few days and the ridiculousness of it all gets me laughing.

"What?"

I'm gasping for breath.

"What?" Mom says, a tentative smile that's kind of a cross between amusement and annoyance playing at her lips.

"He doesn't even like girls," I manage to say in spite of my laughter.

"He seemed like he liked you," she says, looking puzzled.

"No, I mean, he *likes* girls, but not for, you know, to be with them."

Slowly Mom's expression changes. "He's gay?"

I nod my head yes, still laughing, not knowing what's so funny.

Now my mom starts laughing, which gets me going again. "I guess you think I'm as bad as April about jumping to an unfounded conclusion."

I nod my head yes again, laughing harder, barely able to breathe, afraid I'll wet my pants I'm laughing so hard.

Rochelle comes to my room and leans in the doorway. "What's so funny?"

"I don't know," I say, still laughing.

"I want to laugh," she says, which makes us laugh that much harder.

Mom motions Rocky to come sit beside her on the bed. She scoots over a bit and motions to me to sit on the other side. She puts an arm around each of us and pulls us toward her. Rocky is forcing one of those phony laughs that people do when they want to pretend to get a joke. I wipe tears of laughter from my eyes.

"My two babies," Mom sighs. "Not babies anymore."

I lean my head against Mom's shoulder, relieved that the tension between us has lifted.

Kitty perks up her ears and sits stiff and alert. We get suddenly quiet, listening, watching the dog. When Kitty relaxes, we do too.

"I'll be glad when Dad gets home," Mom says. "I've been hearing noises late at night and sometimes I get the strangest feeling that someone's watching the house."

"Too many of those horror stories," I say, referring to my mom's weird tastes in reading.

"I don't think so," Mom says. "I've been reading Stephen King and Dean Koontz for years without hearing noises. Haven't you heard anything?"

I shake my head no, hoping I'm not blushing.

"I did. Just the other night," Rocky says.

"What kind of noises?" Mom asks.

"Sort of like footsteps and breathing."

"Great imagination," I say, sarcastically. I suppose now we shouldn't even breathe when Danny visits late at night.

"You should see the dog Antoinette brought in today," I say, desperate to change the subject.

7

Something about this day, the weather, sitting waiting for the bus, the smog, *something* reminds me of the day Danny's mom died.

I was at school when it happened. As usual April was the newscaster. I've heard older people talk about where they were and what they were doing when they first got word of Kennedy's assassination—the feel of the day, the people around them, all are clear to them. It seems that my memory of the day Danny's mom died will always be that clear to me.

I was waiting for the 117 bus to take me to work. Even though it was only early March, it was typical summer weather, ninety-two degrees and smoggy. I could feel a sting at the back of my throat with each breath of heavy gray air I inhaled. I was reading *The Catcher in the Rye* for my American lit class, and trying to figure out why Holden Caulfield was such an unhappy guy.

Sinclair had asked if I could be at work a little early, to help the health technician get things set up for spaying and neutering. That was fine with me. I was scheduled to assist later, which was also fine with me. I'm not squeamish.

So I was sitting there breathing poison and reading, when a car pulled up to the bus stop. April got out on the passenger side and told me to get in. Usually I don't take orders from April, but on this day she was so intense I didn't even ask any questions. I simply climbed into the back seat. The driver was one of the security guards from school—Narco, kids called him because he was always on the lookout for drugs. His real name was Frank.

April climbed into the back seat next to me and held my hand, tight.

"Something awful has happened," she said, breathless.

In that moment my mind filled with thoughts of tragedies—my mother, Rocky, Kitty, my father, far away in Germany. Or maybe April's mother, or father? In an instant tens of people, maimed, dead, whizzed through my mind. Not one of them was Mrs. Lara, or even Danny.

"She was in the crosswalk and everything," April said, red-faced and teary-eyed.

"Who?"

"Danny's mom. Mrs. Lara. It's really bad."

"What hospital?" Frank said.

"Community," April answered.

Frank took off toward the freeway.

"Will she be okay?"

"I don't know. They said she was critical."

"Who?"

"Alex. He was at Danny's when the call came from the hospital. They asked him to get her family there as soon as he could."

"Where's Danny?"

"They already got him from class and over to the hospital."

"How did you hear?"

"Alex found me in the hall, just before class. He was looking for you. I told him I'd find you."

"God. Where was she?"

"Down near that big nursery, on Seventh."

"But how bad was she hurt?"

"All I know is what I already said. The hospital said her condition was critical, whatever that means."

"It doesn't mean anything good," I said.

Frank turned off the freeway and onto Santa Anita. "Here we are," he said, stopping at the emergency entrance. "Want me to wait for you?"

"No, thanks," I said.

April and I walked through the automatic double doors, into a waiting room. Alex was there, with his head leaning back against the wall, eyes closed. April and I sat down next to him.

"How is she?" I asked.

Alex opened his eyes and looked at me.

"Bad."

"How bad?"

"I don't know. They're in there with her now."

"When did it happen?"

"A couple of hours ago, I guess. It was about one when they called. It was lucky I was there. I'd been staying there all week. I'd washed my gym stuff last night, then forgot it. I went to get it at lunchtime and that's when they called."

We sat for a long time on hard plastic chairs, under fluorescent lights, watching people come and go. I walked out and found a pay phone so I could call work and tell them that I couldn't make it.

"I hope everything's going to be okay," Sinclair said. "Send our best thoughts to Danny and his family."

"Thanks, Sinclair."

I bought a soda and went back to the waiting room. It was nearly dark out when a nurse said we could see the family. She led us to this sort of private place that was carpeted and had upholstered furniture. I got a really bad feeling when I saw that room. Danny and his father were sitting at opposite ends of the couch. His dad was leaning forward, into his arms. Danny was sort of staring at the wall. When he saw me, he just shook his head no.

I sat next to Danny and took his hand. Again he shook his head. Tears rolled down his cheeks.

"No, man," Alex whispered. "No. She was right there this morning, when I was leaving for school."

Mr. Lara looked up at Alex, and then back down again. A nurse came to the doorway.

"Come with me," she said, motioning to Danny's dad. He followed her out of the room and Alex and April both pulled chairs close to where Danny was sitting.

"She was walking across the street, in the crosswalk and everything, and a lady ran right over her—didn't see her, she said."

"Was she drunk?" April asked.

"No, she never drank anything," Danny said.

"She means the driver," I said.

"No. Nothing like that. She had a kid in her car. Maybe she was distracted. I don't know," Danny said, wiping his eyes with the back of his hand. "I don't know."

"Can I go see her?" Alex asked, tears in his eyes, too.

"No, man. You don't want to. She's all messed up," Danny said, letting go with high-pitched little gasping sounds. I put my arm around him, not knowing what to say. Alex came to the other side and put his hand on Danny's shoulder. April sat watching, her eyes, too, filled with tears.

"My dad's signing papers right now, for har . . . har . . ." He stopped and took a deep breath. "Harvesting of organs," he said, convulsing into sobs.

$\textbf{A}$t the service, three days after she died, people talked about what a wonderful friend Irene had been to them. A lot of them were people Danny'd never even heard of before. They talked of how she'd given them plant cuttings, or helped them bring a dying azalea back to life.

Alex stood and told of how he always felt safe with Irene, and knew she'd let him stay whenever things got tough for him. He didn't talk about *why* he needed another place than home—his mean, crazy brother, or his drunk mom, he just said how important Irene had been in his life.

There were pictures of Irene on display at the front of the chapel—wedding pictures with Danny's dad looking young and handsome and happy, next to a broadly smiling young Irene. And family pictures, and pictures that she'd taken of her flower garden in bloom.

There was a whole series of Danny with his mom, taken on the first day of school from kindergarten through high school. The pictures and the talks people gave made me wish I'd known her longer and better.

Danny and his dad both sat stiff and dry-eyed. At the cemetery they each dropped a shovel full of dirt onto the casket, before it was buried in the ground. I was close enough to Danny to hear his whispered promise.

"I won't forget you, Mama. I'll be here every week, no matter what."

After that, he and his dad shook hands with everyone, not saying much, accepting condolences. We stood on the side of the hill, surrounded on all sides by acres and acres of tombstones, looking out over the freeway, the noise of the whizzing cars offering a background rhythm to the prayers of the priest.

But for all of my memories of that day, Danny's controlled sorrow and his father's stiff-backed posture, the pictures, Alex's sweet talk, and the weedless green grass covering rolling hill after rolling hill, what I most remember is the muffled sobbing of the woman in the back row of the chapel—the driver of the car that had taken Irene Lara's life. And I thought of all the lives that had been so drastically changed with her death.

A week after the funeral, late at night, in the car he'd borrowed from his dad, Danny and I made love for the first time since his mother's death. We'd only been with each other, in that way, for a month or so. Always, after we finished, we'd lie together talking about the future, and how much we loved each other. Sometimes we laughed, but neither of us ever cried.

On that night back in March, though, we got together quickly, without much talk. When it was over, Danny clung to me and cried the full cry of a hurt child. I kissed the top of his head and wiped his cheeks. Now every time we make love, he cries when it's over. Maybe the only time he can release his sadness is when we're so close. I'm not sure. I am sure he needs me more than ever since his mom died, and more than ever I want to be there for him. That's what love's about.

In April, Ms. Woods, who knew Danny and I were a couple, called me to her desk after class.

"Why hasn't Daniel returned to school yet?" she'd asked, sounding concerned.

"I'm not sure," I'd said.

"You know, we've got a grief group that meets here—for

students who've experienced the death of a parent or some other important person. It might help."

"I'll tell him."

"I'm sure he could still graduate on time if he came back soon and did some make-up work."

"Okay," I said, eager to get to my next class before the tardy bell.

When I saw Danny later that evening I told him about my conversation with Ms. Woods. Of the possibility of graduating on time, he'd said. "What's the point?" And of the grief group he'd said, "I'll handle it."

"Getting on?" the bus driver says, calling me back from the past. I step onto the bus, fumbling around in my backpack for my bus pass. The driver taps his fingers impatiently on the steering wheel.

"Sorry," I say, showing the pass and finding a seat toward the back.

When I get home there's a message on the machine from Mom to call her at work.

"What's up?" I ask, after I finally press one for the Hamilton Heights branch, press three for accounting, and then press extension 216 for my mom.

"I've been thinking about you all day," Mom says. "And I'm afraid I was a bit harsh about Danny. I know he's been through a very bad time."

"I think he still really misses his mom. And his dad has sort of deserted him as far as caring about him goes. It's like he's a total orphan."

"What you said about me not knowing Danny very well kind of struck home. How would you feel about inviting him over for dinner sometime this week?"

"Sure," I say.

Friday evening we make salad and spaghetti and garlic bread and Danny comes for dinner. It's not a big deal, just one more plate on the table and a fresh tablecloth instead of the three straw placemats that are usually on the table. Well, I guess Rocky thinks it's a big deal because she reeks of my mom's perfume and she's wearing a dress.

Rocky is not what you'd call subtle. As soon as Danny walks through the door she runs up to him. "Smell me," she says.

"Rochelle!" Mom says, pausing over the salad. "That's hardly a polite request."

Danny leans down and smells the spot on Rocky's neck that she's pointing out for him.

"You smell *so* good," Danny says. "Oh, and my heart," he pats his chest in a quick, fluttery motion. "Is that a *love* potion?"

Rochelle blushes and leans closer to Danny.

"Hi, Mrs. Arredondo," Danny says.

"Hi, Danny. Call me Gloria, though, remember? Mrs. Arredondo makes me feel old."

My mom has told him this about a thousand times, but I know how he feels. It's weird calling someone else's parent by their first name, and it's also weird doing the Mr./Mrs. thing.

All through dinner, Kitty rests her head on Danny's knee and looks up at him as if she's not been fed for a week and he is her only hope. Finally, he slips her a piece of garlic bread.

"Now she'll never leave you alone," Mom says. "I've never known a dog to love garlic the way this one does."

"You've never known any other dog," I remind her.

Rochelle finishes her food before anyone else is even half done.

"Come on," she says to Danny, pulling on his arm. "Come play ping-pong with me."

"Rochelle, let Danny finish his dinner in peace," Mom says.

"He's already eaten a lot!" Rocky says.

We laugh, but Danny seems embarrassed. "I never sit at a table and eat dinner anymore," he explains.

"Then you'll have to come more often," Mom says.

Danny helps himself to more spaghetti, then passes the dish toward Mom.

"Don't tempt me! I've got to lose ten pounds before Grant gets back."

"You shouldn't lose weight, Mrs. . . . Gloria," Danny says.

"You're just right."

Mom laughs. "It's that or buy a whole new wardrobe, and I can't afford all new clothes."

"Want to hear my solo?" Rocky asks Danny. "I have to sing a *solo* for the Christmas choir concert," Rocky says, like she hates it. She really loves it, though, because she practices all the time. It's not even Thanksgiving yet, much less Christmas, but judging from Rocky's constant practicing, you'd think the concert was only a day away.

"Rochelle, let Danny eat," Mom says, again.

Danny laughs. "I've been wanting to hear your solo," he says.

"See?" Rocky says to Mom.

Then she starts singing "Oh Holy Night" at the top of her lungs. When she finishes we all clap, but Danny shows the most enthusiasm, probably because he hasn't been hearing "Oh Holy Night" about a thousand times a day.

"I'm good, huh?"

"Yeah," Danny laughs.

"And modest, too," Mom says.

After his third helping of spaghetti, Danny wipes his mouth and sets his napkin on the table beside his plate.

"That was really good," he says. "Thank you."

Mom looks at him intently, like she's adjusting her vision.

"How *are* things with you these days, Danny?"

The other night she was talking to me like Danny was the scourge of the universe and tonight she's all friendly. Go figure.

"Things are cool," Danny says. "School, job hunting, same old stuff."

"Are you in school now?" Mom asks.

He nods his head yes. "Finishing my high school equivalency, then I can start city college—right now I really need a job, though."

This is news to me! The last I'd heard Danny wasn't going to school at all. I look at him, trying to make sense of what he's just said, but he doesn't look my way.

"Do you know anything about carpentry?" Mom asks.

"A little. When I was younger my dad used to take me out on jobs with him. He taught me how to do some stuff," Danny says.

"We've got a little work that needs to be done around here. Are you interested?"

"Sure."

Mom starts showing Danny all of these things that have been bugging her, like where the bookshelves have been loose since the last earthquake, and the section of back fence that needs to be rebuilt.

"Can you do it?" Mom asks.

"No problem," Danny says.

They arrange a schedule and Mom says she'll pay Danny six dollars an hour, then she puts her dishes into the dishwasher and goes into the other room to watch the news.

Danny takes one of those really little bottles of Jack Daniels whiskey from his pocket and pours some into his glass of water.

"Want some?" he asks, quietly.

"No," I say, surprised by what I've just seen.

Danny pours the rest of the contents into his glass and puts the empty bottle back in his pocket.

"Just a little something to keep me warm on the way home," he explains. "No big deal."

I'm probably looking at him strangely. I can't tell how I look, but I know I'm feeling strange.

"Free," he says, pulling four other little bottles, all Jack Daniels, from various pockets. "Gladys knows a guy who works for the airlines . . ."

"Gladys?"

"You know, Alex's mom. Anyway, this guy brings stuff to her all the time. She keeps all the vodka for herself, but she gives the rest away," he laughs. "She's a trip."

"She helped you out the other day," I remind him.

"For sure. You know my dad's never gone to the police station to clear things up? He's going to make us go through the whole hearing business, maybe even get us put on probation, with a record. I can't believe that shit."

"Have you talked to him?"

"Who can talk to him? He's an asshole."

"But you used to talk to him, didn't you? I mean, you said tonight he used to take you with him on his jobs sometimes."

"Yeah, I don't get it either. When my mom was around my dad

acted normal, but as soon as she died he turned into the biggest asshole in the world, always on my case about every little thing—my pants are too baggy, my haircut's not normal, I'm a slob—I probably don't even breathe right as far as he's concerned."

"Maybe he really misses your mom, too."

"Right. The grass wasn't even growing over her grave before he started having whores to the house."

Danny's whole body changes when he talks about his father. His face looks drawn and tight.

"I don't give a shit about him, anyway." He adds a little more Jack Daniels to his water, which now looks sort of brownish. "I give a shit about you, though," he says.

"How romantic," I tell him, laughing.

He pulls me toward him and kisses the top of my head. I lift my head, to kiss his lips, but we're interrupted by Mom yelling at us above the noise of the TV, "Don't forget to rinse your dishes and put them in the dishwasher when you're finished."

Danny laughs, but then he gets this sad look on his face.

"What?" I say.

"What? What do you mean?" he asks.

"What are you looking so sad about?"

He shakes his head. "I don't know. Sometimes I miss having a mom to tell me what to do. There's nobody now to tell me to rinse my dishes and put them in the dishwasher."

"Somebody just did," I say.

"Yeah, but you know what I mean. It's not the same."

He downs his whiskey-laced drink, puts the glass and his plate in the dishwasher and gives me a quick, distant kiss.

"I gotta go," he says, and he's out the door before I can even say good-bye.

In my room I wait for a tapping at my window, but it doesn't come. Danny didn't even say when he'd see me again. He does that sometimes. He'll tell me something private, like he misses his mom, but then after he says it, he acts sort of mad, or like he has no feelings. He isn't always easy to understand.

I force Danny out of my mind and concentrate on English and

biology. I'll save calculus for the weekend.

In the story about Gregor Samsa, when he tries to talk to his family, and the manager from his work, he scares them because he sounds like an animal. And then when they see him, they all go nuts. And all the time he's trying to meet his responsibilities, no matter how he looks or feels.

Even though I want to be a vet, I've never been very interested in bugs. But the next time I see one, I'm going to be extra careful not to step on it, because now I know how Gregor feels.

Sometime around three in the morning, after I've been asleep for hours, Rocky comes and gets in bed with me. She snuggles up close to me and asks, "Are you glad I'm your sister?"

"Yeah," I mumble, not wanting to wake up for her questions.

"I'm glad you're my sister," she says.

I wonder how she'd feel if I turned into a giant beetle and oozed a sticky brown substance? Would she still be glad I was her sister?

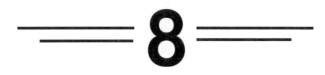
First thing I do when I get to the Humane Society Saturday morning is check on the dog Antoinette brought in. She is so still I'm afraid to take a closer look, but then, seeing the movement of her upper body, I walk softly to her cage.

"Hey, Beauty," I say.

She lifts her head slightly. I open the cage and reach in to pet her. It doesn't look as if she's eaten much. I take a bit of food in my fingers and hold it under her nose. She sniffs at it.

"Come on, get strong," I tell her.

She licks the food and I offer her a few more bites. I know not to try to feed her too much at one time because her poor stomach probably couldn't handle it. I pull the water dish close to her but she puts her head back down on her paws. I go to the supply room kitchen, get some ice from the freezer and put it in a plastic freezer bag. Then I bang the bag with a hammer until the ice is in small chips and take it back to her cage. I take a small chip and gently push it into her mouth, then another. Looking at me with dull, sad eyes, she taps her tail weakly, twice.

"Makes you wonder about people, doesn't it?"

It's Dr. Franz, in her green lab coat. She checks the dog's eyes, mouth, skin, listens to her heart, and jots some notes on her information card.

"Will she be okay?"

"Hard to tell. Malnourished, dehydrated, miserable skin condition. I don't see evidence of any major internal disease. Physically, she has a strong heartbeat, but I'm not sure how strong her heart is for life anymore . . . Want to make the rounds with me?"

"Sure," I say. "Bye, Beauty," I say to the dog.

"Beauty?" Dr. Franz smiles, looking at the skinny, mangy dog. "That's a perfect name for her," she says, writing "Beauty" on the information card that's attached to the cage.

"And her owner's the beast," Antoinette says, as she pauses at the cage to look in on the dog.

Helping mix vaccines for the newer "residents" and hearing Dr. Franz talk about each animal as she makes the rounds is one of my favorite things to do around here. We start with the newly arrived strays.

"Sometimes I think I should open a nicely decorated clinic in Sycamore Hills and work with pampered poodles and Persian cats and not think about animals that are neglected or abused. I'd never have to end another healthy animal's life just because no one wanted to give it a home."

Dr. Franz is nearly six feet tall. She's older than my mom and younger than my gramma. I guess that makes her somewhere between forty and sixty-five. Her hair is gray and it's only about an inch long. I've never seen her wear anything but jeans and a T-shirt and the green lab coat she wears when she's working with the animals. When it's cold she wears a down jacket that she's had since college. I'm not sure she'd fit in with the Sycamore Hills crowd, but I don't think it's a serious consideration anyway.

She marks a card on the cage of a young Labrador retriever, scheduling him for neutering the next day.

"I'd make more money," Dr. Franz says, moving on to the next cage.

I follow along in silence. One thing I learned early on here is that there are days when some of the staff get all down and it's best not to bug them with questions or try to talk to them on those days. They sort of protect me, and the volunteers, too, as far as euthanasia goes. If we ask what happened to one of our favorite dogs, or cats, or rabbits, that's no longer in its cage, staff members always say "adopted."

That's true about eighty percent of the time, but it's not always true. Most people don't want to think about a healthy, homeless animal being put to death, so they accept the "adopted" answer without further questions. I can tell, though, whether the staff member is telling the truth, or just saying what they know people want to hear. "Really?" I ask, when I see the sadness creep around the eyes and mouth. And a shake of the head, or silence, tells me that "adoption" was a euphemism for a quick, painless death.

The first time I held an animal that was being put down, I wasn't sure I could stand it. But I knew I needed to see the whole picture, not just the easy part.

She was an old cocker with health problems, black, with gentle eyes, but not the kind of animal that gets adopted. She was trying to lick my face when she got the injection. Five seconds later she was dead. I managed not to cry until later, when I was with Danny, and he held me in his arms.

"You helped that old dog into heaven," he'd told me.

I hope that's true, but I doubt it. I think I just helped her out of the world in the kindest way possible.

Dr. Franz's mood lightens with the puppies who clamber in heaps over their brothers and sisters—healthy, cute, energetic puppies—the kind who always get adopted—really adopted.

"Pay no attention to me," she says. "I love this work, and it's important. Maybe I'll leave the poodles and Persians of Sycamore Hills to you."

I laugh.

"Have you sent your college applications off yet?"

"I've been wanting to talk with you about that. Would you write a recommendation for me, for Davis?"

"Of course. Just bring me the forms."

The screeching call of the caracara fills the air. "I guess you got a recommendation from Toopee," Dr. Franz says.

Back in the infirmary we pause again at Beauty's cage. I hand-feed her a few more bites.

"Why don't you take over with this one?" Dr. Franz says.

"How?"

"Keep a check on her diet, regulate the mange medication, get rid of the fleas, socialize her, set her up for vaccinations, and spaying, when the time is right. You can handle that."

"Yeah, okay," I say, pleased with the assignment.

Early in the afternoon Sinclair and I go to the back parking lot with cleaning supplies for the mobile pet adoption van. We clean and disinfect all of the cages and wipe down all of the hard surfaces inside the van, including the floor.

"Here, I'll buy you a soda," Sinclair jokes, taking two cans of cola from the van's tiny refrigerator and handing me one.

We step outside and lean against the van, drinking soda and talking. I see a familiar looking Honda turn into the alley. It's Alex and Danny. They park next to the van and Danny gets out. There's some older guy in the back seat—someone I've never seen before.

"Hey, Pups," Danny smiles.

"Hi." I stand and walk toward him.

"Hi, Daniel," Sinclair says, reaching toward him.

"Hey, Sinclair," Danny says, shaking Sinclair's hand, then turning toward me.

"I need to talk to you," he says.

"I'll see you inside," Sinclair says, as he walks through the back gate near the kennels. "'Bye, 'bye," he says to Danny.

"Listen, Pups. Something came up. You know how I was supposed to start work on your fence this afternoon?"

"Yeah, Mom was off to the lumberyard for materials before I even left for work this morning."

"Well, something's come up. I need to go take care of some business with Alex and his brother."

"His brother?"

"Yeah, Joey," Danny says, nodding toward the car. "He got home last night. They let him out early—overcrowded facilities—they had to make room for the new ones coming in—kind of like here, only he didn't get 'adopted,' they just let him loose," Danny laughs.

"What am I supposed to tell Mom?" I say. "Why don't you call her?"

"No, Pups, I've got to hurry. You can tell her, can't you?" Danny says, looking at me intently. "This is important. I don't have time to explain it all now, just believe me, it's important."

Joey gets out of the back seat of the car, gives Danny a look that oozes meanness, then sits down in the front seat, leaving the door open. I see that he is taller than Alex, almost as tall as Danny. And the tight T-shirt he's wearing shows muscles that must be the result of years of working out with weights. His hair is light like Alex's, and cropped short.

"Let's go," he yells.

"Okay, okay," Danny yells back.

He leans down and kisses me. "I'll be back in a couple of days," he says. "Tell your mom I can for sure start work on the fence Tuesday morning."

Joey leans out the window. "Say bye-bye," he yells at Danny, mimicking Sinclair's tone and waving a limp wrist.

"*What* is *his* problem?" I ask Danny, loud enough for Joey to hear.

"Don't worry about it," Danny says. "Listen. I know I haven't been a great boyfriend lately, but I promise I'm going to make it all up to you when I get back. You'll see. We'll do something really special. Like Tuesday night, after I finish your mom's fence. Okay?"

"You don't have time to get any right now!" Joey yells.

"Is that guy totally uncivilized, or what?"

"I've gotta go." Danny kisses me, quickly, runs back to the car, jumps in, and Alex speeds off down the alley.

Great. My mom starts liking Danny, for about a day, and now he's not going to show up to do the work for her the way he'd promised? To quote April's grandmother, this will go over like a fart in church.

I check back on Beauty, and hand-feed her a bit more. Is it my imagination or are her eyes a little brighter?

"You've got to work a little harder at eating," I tell her.

I take my keys to the office and sign out. I *dread* telling my mom that Danny won't be there until Tuesday.

Over the weekend, while I'm studying, or walking around the mall with April, or watching a video with Rocky, Danny is on my mind. I wonder where he is? And why was he so mysterious? And has he totally forgotten that our one-year anniversary is practically here?

When I get home from school on Tuesday, there's a message on the machine for me to call Mom at her work.

"What happened to Danny?" she says, not even bothering with "hello" when she hears my voice.

"I don't know. I thought he'd be here," I say.

"Dad will be home soon, and I want things to be in order. I was planning on Danny doing what he said he'd do."

"He's not usually like this."

"I took a long break this morning and drove home, expecting Danny to be there. I wanted to be sure he had everything he needed. I waited around as long as I could. He didn't show and he didn't call."

It really upsets my mom when people tell her they'll do something and then don't follow through.

"I could have hired the man who did some work for us last summer, but I thought I could help Danny out. I know he needs the money."

"I'm sure he's got a good reason, Mom," I say, hoping it's true.

"Well, surely he could have called," Mom says.

"I'm sorry," I say, and then wonder why *I'm* apologizing for Danny. I haven't done anything wrong.

After the phone call with Mom, I call Alex's house. His mom answers. Neither Danny nor Alex is there.

"I don't know where Danny is," Mrs. Kendall says. "I can't even keep up with Alex, much less all of his friends that are in and out of here."

Her voice is coarse and her words are slurred.

"Well, do you know where they might be?" I ask.

"No. Joey wanted them to take him somewhere—I've hardly seen anything of them since I got Joey from camp."

"Well, would you have Danny call me if you see him? This is

Erica."

"Sure, Honey," she says, but I don't have much faith that Danny will get my message.

I get Kitty's leash and she runs to the door, then back to me. I catch her and manage to hook the leash onto her collar and we start walking. We stop at the park and sit under this huge oak tree that must be about a thousand years old. Kitty nudges me with her nose, wanting to move on.

"What's your hurry?" I say, holding her face between my hands and looking deep into her eyes. She doesn't answer.

"Sit," I say, and she does. I've taught her all that stuff, sit, stay, heel, and I did it without ever hitting her.

"You know, you've got a really good life in comparison to some poor dogs," I tell her, thinking of Beauty. "I'm glad *I* got you, and that you didn't go to some stupid jerk who wouldn't even see to it that you had food and water."

We sit side by side for awhile. I don't know what Kitty thinks about, but I think about Danny. I get mad. Is this his idea of making things up to me? I'm sitting in the park with my dog at a time we were supposed to be doing something special? Not only has he disappeared for days without even a phone call, he messed up with my mom. That's *really* bad. She'll probably never let me forget it and it's not even my fault.

All the times Danny's let me down start marching around in my brain—the times I've sat waiting for him when he said he'd meet me after school, then didn't show, or when he said he'd call, and didn't. Other things, too, like borrowing money and not paying it back, like he just took for granted that whatever he needed it for was more important than what I needed it for.

And how we talk and talk about his stuff, but as soon as I start to tell him any of my problems, he has to hang up the phone. Like last week, after I'd listened all about his dad, and the police, and everything, and as soon as I tried to tell him how mad my mom was, and how *I* was feeling, he had to go.

I scratch Kitty behind the ear. "Maybe Danny doesn't really care about me," I say, and I get a funny, hollow feeling deep inside.

Then I start worrying. How can I be thinking such bad things about Danny when maybe something terrible has happened to him. Maybe he was in a bad accident and he didn't have any I.D. on him. He's somewhere dying and I'm mad at him because he didn't show up today?

I get up and start running back home, Kitty loping along at my side. Maybe Danny's called while I was gone, or maybe someone else, a doctor from the hospital where Danny might be. I picture the waiting room of the hospital where Danny's mother died. Maybe sudden tragic death runs in families.

The rest of the week is kind of a blur, trying to do what I need to do at school, and at work, but always, always, thinking of Danny. Television reports of a freeway shooting leave me trembling with the news that two eighteen-year-olds are in critical condition. Their names won't be released until the next of kin is notified. I call all of the emergency treatment centers in Los Angeles County and ask if anyone meeting Danny's description has been brought in. The answer is no, every place I call, but sometimes I think they don't even check.

The best thing that happens this week is that, on Thursday, when I walk into the infirmary, Beauty stands and wags her tail when she hears my voice.

"Wow! You ate all your food already, too," I say.

She wags her tail and takes a drink of water, as if to say, "Look at what else I can do now."

I give her another flea powder treatment and check the mange. Then I put her into another cage and clean hers thoroughly. When I finish, I put a fresh mat in for her to sleep on, and give her my usual pep talk.

By Friday night, when I still haven't heard from Danny, I'm kind of going nuts. I think about that Jeffrey Dahmer creep who kidnapped and tortured and killed all those guys and I get scared for Danny. It's got to be something awful or he'd have called me.

Alex hasn't been around either. I've called over there every day.

Alex's mom doesn't seem to be worried—says they're just boys, sowing their wild oats, whatever she means by that. But I know something awful has happened.

I even call Danny's dad, who just says, "He'll turn up, like a bad penny. You can depend on that," and then he hangs up.

CHAPTER

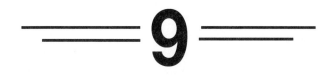

"Erica!"

I turn to see Danny and Alex, leaning against the wall of the Humane Society when I leave work Monday evening.

"Danny! Where've you been?"

"He's been to London, to visit the queen," Alex says, laughing a strange, high-pitched laugh.

Danny walks over to me and puts his arms around me.

"I've missed you, Pups," he says.

I'm so relieved, I start crying. "But where have you been?"

"Pussycat, Pussycat, where have you been?" Alex giggles.

Danny turns toward Alex. "Shut up," he says.

"I told you I was going with Alex and Joey to take care of some business."

"You also told me you'd be back on Tuesday, and you'd do that work for my mom!"

"Shhh," he says, kissing me and holding me tight. "I'll tell you all about it later. Alex has to get home, then I can use his car. Come with me."

"I can't. Mom's waiting for me out back."

"Tell her I'll bring you home later."

"She's mad at you."

"Why?"

"'Cause you didn't show up to do that work. Twice."

"Tell her April will bring you home then, if she's mad at me. But tell her something. I'll be waiting for you right here."

I wipe my eyes and walk around the corner to where Mom is waiting in the car with Kitty.

"Danny's here, Mom. I'm going out with him for awhile and then he'll bring me home."

"Where's *he* been?"

"I don't know."

"Well, I don't think you should drop everything to go with Danny when he hasn't even had the courtesy to call all week long, and when he's been so completely irresponsible about keeping his agreements with me."

"Mom, please," I say. "I need to talk to him."

She looks at me and softens. "Of course you do. Don't be too late."

I dump my books in her car, then go back to meet Danny.

"We'll drop Alex off at home," Danny says, putting his arm around me and walking with me to Alex's car. Alex is slumped down in the back seat, eyes half closed, next to Joey, who appears to be sound asleep. Danny gets into the driver's seat and I get in on the other side. The inside of the car smells like pot.

"Keys?" Danny says, reaching back toward Alex.

Alex fumbles around, then finds his keys in his jacket pocket and hands them up to Danny. Besides his car keys, there are a couple of other keys, probably house keys, and a round, silver emblem with a marijuana leaf engraved on it.

"Gina's pissed, too," Alex giggles. "But business is business."

I don't say anything and neither does Danny. I'll be glad when Alex and Joey are out of the car. Tonight is one of those times I don't like Alex, and I have a feeling there will never be a time when I like Joey.

Headlights of cars and streetlights along the way cast light and shadows on Danny's face. He looks so good to me, familiar and safe and strong.

After we drop Alex and Joey off we drive to McDonald's.

"I haven't eaten since early this morning," Danny says as we wait in line in the drive-thru lane. "My stomach's complaining. How about you?"

"I'm hungry, too," I say, suddenly realizing I've hardly eaten anything for a week.

"I don't have much money on me."

"I've got some."

"Enough?"

"Yeah. I got paid yesterday," I tell him.

"I can pay you back pretty soon," Danny says. "Not just for tonight, but all the other money I've borrowed from you, too."

"Did you find a job?" I ask.

"Sort of."

He orders two hamburgers and two large fries and I order a salad. We both get sodas. I hand Danny $11.

"Where?" I ask him.

"What?" he says.

"The job?"

"Oh, I'll tell you about it later."

After we get our food, he drives down to the cemetery where his mom is buried.

"I haven't visited in over two weeks," he says. "You don't mind, do you?"

"No," I say, knowing how stressed Danny gets when he goes more than a week between visits to his mother's grave. I respect Danny for keeping his word to his mother, even if she didn't hear him make the promise to her.

We sit in the car, eating. Danny reaches into the glove compartment and pulls out a little Jack Daniels bottle, then empties it into his soda.

"There's more. Want some?" he says, holding the empty bottle up.

"You know I don't drink that stuff," I tell him. "I don't even like it when you do, so why offer?"

"I'm just being polite. You don't have to get all mad about it."

"I *am* mad," I yell at him. "You totally disappeared for days. We had plans for last Tuesday, including you were going to work for my mom, and then we were going out, 'someplace special,' you said, but you didn't show, you didn't call, I didn't even know if you were dead or alive, and then you show up like nothing's happened?"

For an instant he looks at me as if I'm an absolute stranger. Then he yells back, "I *said* I had some business to take care of. Okay? I need money, and I had a chance to make a lot more than six dollars an hour being your mom's little handyman!"

"You could at least have called Tuesday to say you couldn't make it!"

"Don't nag me, Erica! You sound like my dad! I won't take that shit from any girl!"

He reaches into the glove compartment, opens another Jack Daniels and takes a swallow, straight.

I'm trying to choke back tears but I can't. "I'm not *any* girl! How can you say that? You say you love me, but you sure don't act like it sometimes!"

Danny jumps out of the car and slams the door, hard. He takes a few steps away, turns back, jerks open the car door, gets his food, reaches past me to the glove compartment and grabs a handful of the little bottles, then slams the door again with such force I think the window will break. I'm crying so hard now I'm blubbering.

I watch as Danny walks across the dimly lit cemetery to where his mother is buried. My hands shake as I dig a paper napkin from the bag my salad came in. I blow my nose and try to stop crying. At this rate I'll need about a hundred more paper napkins.

I feel all trembly inside. Danny and I have never really fought like this before. In the distance I see him squatting down by Mrs. Lara's tombstone. Why did I get him mad? If I'd just have acted like everything was okay, then it probably would have been. But I have a right to be mad! He used to call me all the time, and he was always there when he said he'd be. What's happened? . . . Maybe Danny doesn't love me anymore.

With that thought my tears come faster. I can barely catch my breath. The windows are so steamy now I can't see out. I wipe the one opposite me with my sleeve. Danny is still sitting in exactly the same place he was before. I wish he'd come back.

I've been here with him before. If we come in the daytime I bring flowers from our yard and place them at Mrs. Lara's grave. But when he comes at night I know he wants to be alone with his mom and I wait in the car. Usually he doesn't stay long.

"I can't lose touch," is what he says about these visits.

$\mathbf{H}$e's been out there at least twenty minutes. I'm sitting in the car, lonely and cold, wondering if Danny's ever coming back. My nose is still runny from crying and I've used up all of the napkins. I rummage around in Alex's glove compartment for tissues. There's nothing but about six more of the little bottles, a screwdriver, and a dirty old rag.

I look in the side pockets of both doors. I wipe my nose on my sleeve. Gross! I feel around under the driver's seat, which is where my mom always stashes those little packets of tissue.

Something feels kind of bumpy, so I stick my hand under the carpet. I touch a package that I hope is tissue and pull it out. What is it? I switch on the light in the car and see that it's a zip-lock sandwich bag filled with something that looks like crushed leaves or . . . marijuana.

I quickly turn off the light and put the baggy back under the seat where I found it and feel around for more. There must be about ten packages under both seats. I wonder if Danny knows they're there, or if it's all Alex and Joey's doing? It *is* Alex's car. Danny doesn't even smoke weed anymore. At least that's what he says. Maybe it's not even weed. Maybe it's something else. Like Alex is carrying baggies of oregano around? He's going to make tubs of spaghetti sauce? No. It's got to be weed. I don't use it but I know what it looks like.

I know Alex smokes, and I know the rumors about all the partying that goes on at Alex's house. But I've never heard anything about Alex dealing. Smoking it and dealing it are whole different things.

I think about how I'm always accusing April of jumping to unfounded conclusions, and she's always accusing me of not facing things. I wonder what story April would come up with if *she'd* found the baggies. She'd probably be convinced that Alex and Danny and Joey were part of a big drug ring or something.

I'm *freezing*, sitting here waiting for Danny. He's so inconsiderate! I'm really getting sick of being treated like this. I'll go tell him to take me home, tell him he can just forget about me, he won't have to hear my "nagging" anymore.

I get out of the car and start walking over to where Danny is sitting. There are plenty of guys around. I don't need Danny Lara.

I wipe my eyes. I wish I could stop crying before Danny sees me. I hold my breath and walk.

When I get to Mrs. Lara's place I stand over Danny and demand, "Take me home now."

Danny looks up. He looks so sad, and I can see that he's been crying, too. He reaches for my hand and pulls me down beside him, wrapping his arms tightly around me.

"Sorry. I'm sorry, Erica," he whispers. "I need you so much, don't be mad. Please. I love you." He is shivering hard, and I feel his tears against my cheeks.

The hard rock of anger inside me dissolves and my tears flow harder than ever.

"I love you, too," I tell him, clinging tightly, trying to get closer, scared to think how mad we'd been.

"I've been talking to my mom about us," he says. "About a week before she died, she told me she thought you were good for me, and that I should hold on to you. She was right. I know she was right."

I lean my head against Danny's chest and listen. Each time he tells me about how his mom said I was good for him, it's like he thinks he's telling me for the first time. He's told me that about twenty times since she died, but I never get tired of hearing it. It made a big impression on him.

"I told my mom how stupid I'd been, just to stay away without calling you or anything," Danny says, turning to the side and running his hand lightly across his mom's tombstone, then holding me close again. We are both crying.

"If I lost you, my life wouldn't be worth shit," he says. "I'd be totally alone."

"I started thinking maybe you'd been tortured and murdered by one of those Jeffrey Dahmer kind of guys. I couldn't stand thinking you were hurt, or dead . . ."

"I'll do better, you'll see. I'll make it up to you."

I remember how he told me that just last week, and then he disappeared.

"Let's go," he says. "We're both freezing out here." He kisses me long, pushing his tongue gently past my parted lips. He tastes of whiskey.

I walk a little ways away from him to give him a chance to say good-bye to his mom in private. He gathers up his trash, hamburger wrappers and empty bottles, then we walk back to the car together. We drive to an all-night market.

"Can I borrow another five? I can pay you back tomorrow for sure."

I take my last five dollar bill from my backpack and hand it to Danny.

"For supplies," Danny says, as he gets out of the car.

I know he's buying condoms and foam. When he gets back in the car he slides the paper bag under the seat, and I'm reminded of what else is there. For a moment I think I'll ask about the baggies, but all I want to do is feel Danny's presence and his love. I don't want to talk about anything for now.

We drive to this private place we know about, behind an old, deserted hotel that's surrounded by huge trees and away from traffic or street lights. We park and sit for awhile.

"I wish we could live in this old place, just you and me, away from everyone else in the world," Danny says.

I kiss him, first on the forehead, then the cheek, then the lips. I feel his breathing quicken, and lean toward him. He reaches under my sweater and unfastens my bra.

"Your hands are cold," I whisper.

"But the rest of me is very warm," he says, kissing my neck in a way that sends chills through my body.

"Come on," he says, "let's get in back, where we can stretch out better."

$\mathbf{W}$e lie half-dressed, close to each other, breathing in and out in an identical, steady rhythm, after having made quick, awkward love.

"I was so worried," I say.

"I wasn't thinking. Joey and Alex had a chance to make some money, and they let me in on it. Joey said we had to move fast, though. I just took off with them."

"Where did you go?"

There's a long pause, then Danny says, "Just across the border, near where their uncle lives."

"For a job?"

"Sort of," he says, kissing me. "Listen, I'm not supposed to be telling you any of this. Joey would shit if he knew I'd even told you this much. Just love me," he says. "Don't ever stop loving me."

"I do. I won't."

"Promise?"

"Promise."

We hang on to each other, close and secure, finally warm. After a long time, I say what I can't stop thinking about.

"I was looking for tissues when you were at your mom's grave. What's with all the baggies?"

"Erica . . . it's just free enterprise, you know, capitalism and all that. It's a chance to make some bucks."

"It's illegal."

"It's only marijuana. Joey's back, and he says I've got to get out."

"What's Alex say? Or his mom?"

"You don't understand. It's like everything's changed over there now that Joey's home . . . Alex and I both are getting out of there, we just need some money for a deposit on a place. Just this one time is all."

"This is stupid! What if you get caught?"

"We won't. Joey knows what he's doing."

"Danny! Joey's just out of prison! If he knows so much, why has he been locked up all this time?"

"This is different," Danny says. "And it wasn't prison. It was a Youth Authority camp."

"Did he have to stay there all the time?"

"Yeah. But it was a camp."

"It was prison."

"Whatever," Danny says, starting the engine and pulling out the dirt drive onto the street. We drive in silence to my house, the distance between us filling the car.

CHAPTER

10

For days Danny and I don't see each other. Finally, I call Alex's. Joey answers.

"Is Danny there?" I ask.

"No," he says.

"Would you ask him to call me when he gets back?"

"If I remember," he says.

I hang up.

At the Humane Society I concentrate on Beauty. Now she stands and wags her tail, full out, when I walk through the infirmary doors. I take her to the big dirt pen and walk her on a leash, then play ball with her. She's exhausted after fetching the ball twice. Quite a difference from Kitty, but quite a different life Beauty has led, too. I treat her mange. The flea problem is almost under control.

Beauty's become a favorite here, with Antoinette stopping to see her every day, and Sinclair. I think she's mostly border collie, because of her size, and because of her black coat with white markings.

"You need to do something about that *hair*," Sinclair tells her, primping his own. "Take a lesson from the proud owner of *this* head of hair," he says, pointing at me as if Beauty is actually following what he's saying.

Early, early one morning, about a week after the night Danny and I visited the cemetery, there's a tapping at my window. At first the sound seems to be part of a dream in which I'm on a slow moving train, late, in a hurry, why is the train moving so slowly, click . . . click . . . click . . . along the rails, then a little faster, clickety-clickety-clickety.

I awaken from my dream to a real life noise, the tapping on glass. Groggy, I stumble out of bed and peer out the window, then open it a crack.

"Can I come in?" Danny asks.

I open the window wider and he crawls through. He kisses me on the forehead, tentatively, then the lips. I get a taste of stale alcohol.

"I'm sorry, Pups," he whispers. "Please don't stop loving me. Everything's going to be okay. I promise."

"I don't understand what's happening with us," I whisper.

"It's me. It's my fault. Don't give up on me," he says.

I hug him, hard, so relieved to again feel him close to me. He eases his shoes off and pulls me back to the bed.

"I want so much to always be with you. When I'm with you, everything's okay, and when I'm not, it's shit."

He kisses me again, then goes to my closet and gets the foam and condom, slipping them under the pillow the way we always do.

"Just hold me for awhile," I say.

Usually Danny's sort of in a hurry for sex after the first kiss, but tonight he holds me close, not pushing for more. I rest my head on his chest and feel his breathing become deeper, slower, and I know he's asleep. I drift off, too, comfortable in his warmth.

Neither of us hears anything until Rochelle yells, "Danny!"

I wake in an instant and clap my hand over her mouth. "Shhh!"

Danny jumps up and closes the door, grabs his shoes, and climbs out the window so fast I hardly know what's happening.

"Shhh!" I say again, easing my hand from my sister's mouth. "Erica?"

I hear Mom shuffling barefoot down the hallway.

"Are you okay?"

"Rocky had a bad dream," I say.

Mom opens the door and looks in. My heart is beating fast.

Please, please, please, keep your mouth shut, Rocky, I silently beg her.

"Are you okay now, Honey?" Mom says, sitting on the edge of the bed.

"She's fine," I say, not giving Rocky a chance to talk. "She can sleep with me. She won't be scared anymore, will you?"

Rocky just nods, looking at me strangely. Mom gets a funny look on her face, too, when she leans down to tuck Rocky in. She runs her hand across the pillow where Danny's head was resting just moments ago. Has she noticed something?

When Mom leaves the room I say to Rocky, "Danny wasn't here, do you understand? You didn't see him, and he wasn't here."

"He was too!"

"Shhhh! What I mean is, I want you to forget it."

"Why?"

"Because Mom would totally freak out if she knew Danny was here like this. And she'd ground me forever. And *you'd* have to quit choir because she'd never let me use the car again and there wouldn't be anyone to pick you up when practice is over."

She's giving me this look, like maybe she'll run down the hall right now and tell Mom, or maybe she won't. But I can see the thing about choir practice got her, because she *loves* being in the school choir.

"Listen, Rochelle. I'm serious. Mom would go nuts if you told her."

"Why? Because Danny's your *husband*? Because if you sleep in the same bed it means you're married?"

"Shhh! She wouldn't understand, that's all. Just remember about choir practice," I tell her. "Now go back to bed."

"No. I'm sleeping with you. That's what you told Mom."

Sometimes she is *so* frustrating! "Okay, sleep here then, but I'm going to sleep right now, so you'd better, too."

Rochelle puts her head down on the pillow, then rises up again. "What's wrong?"

"Your pillow smells like Danny," she says, turning it over on the other side. "What's *this*?"

She's holding the foil-wrapped condom that was under the pillow. I grab it from her and close my hand around it, at the same time leaning hard on the pillow so she won't discover the can of foam.

"It's nothing. A breath mint," I tell her.

"I want it. I've got a bad taste in my mouth."

"You can't have it. I'm saving it for Danny."

"I WANT IT! GIVE IT TO ME OR I'LL TELL MOM DANNY WAS HERE!"

"Shut up! Please, Rocky, just shut up and go to sleep."

"GIRLS!" Mom yells at us from her bedroom.

"See! You woke Mom up again."

"I don't care. I want the candy."

"You're not going to get it. And you'd better remember about choir practice, too! Now stop talking stupid and go to sleep," I whisper.

She turns on her side.

"I hate you," she says, lying rigid with her back to me. But then, it can't be more than five minutes, she is sound asleep. I lie wide awake though, worrying about what could happen. Rochelle isn't that great at keeping a secret, and my mom would go into immediate orbit if she knew Danny was in bed with me, especially since she now thinks he's the biggest flake in the world.

In the morning Mom, Rochelle and I stop at Starbuck's for juice and scones. Well, my mom gets some heavy-duty coffee stuff, but Rocky and I get juice. It's my one day a week to get the car, the day I pick Rocky up from choir. So I take Mom to work and then the car's mine for the day.

"What was the problem with you two last night?" Mom asks.

"Nothing, just one of Rocky's nightmares." I answer quickly, hoping my sister will keep quiet.

"I thought I heard something outside again last night. Did you hear anything?"

"No," I say.

Rocky is busy picking raisins out of her scone and doesn't seem to be paying any attention to what Mom and I are talking about.

"I'm thinking maybe we should get an alarm system," Mom says.

"Mom, you're getting all upset over nothing."

"Maybe," she says, then gets out of the car at the five-story office building where she works for a property management company. This is the tallest building in Hamilton Heights, and one of the newest. Just as I pull away from the curb Rochelle yells "Stop!"

I slam on the brakes.

"What?"

"My lunch money," she says, and runs from the car yelling at Mom.

Mom turns at the top of the steps to the building and watches Rochelle, smiling.

"Lunch!" Rochelle yells.

Mom reaches into her purse and pulls out some money, hands it to Rocky and kisses her on the cheek. She smiles and waves at me, then turns and goes into the building. Dressed in a business suit, with hose and medium-high heels, Mom looks very professional. She looks younger than most moms, too, maybe because she's so active.

I love my mom and I don't feel very good about keeping secrets from her. Well, I'm sure she has some secrets from me, too. But I've really never kept much from her, until Danny.

11

As soon as Rocky and I walk into the house after I pick her up from choir practice, I know my dad is home.

"Daddy!" I yell.

Rochelle looks at me like I'm nuts, but I *know* he's here because I got a whiff of English Leather aftershave as soon as I opened the door.

He comes hurrying from the kitchen and gathers us both in his arms at the same time, laughing, then pushing us away and looking from one to the other.

"Rochelle, you've grown a foot since summer, and Erica, you just keep getting prettier and prettier. Let me check out your biceps, E.J." he says, using the nickname only he uses for me.

Rochelle and I both pull up our sleeves and flex our muscles. Dad has been checking our biceps for as long as I can remember. He always says pretty is nice but strong is necessary.

"Lookin' good," he says, walking back into the kitchen where he's got a sandwich and a big glass of milk. "Boy, am I glad to be home for awhile."

One thing about being in the army is that my dad stays in shape. April's dad already has a big pot belly, and so does Mr. Lara. But my dad still looks trim—no belly hanging over his belt. As far as coloring goes, he's the one I take after—dark eyes, black hair, olive skin.

Rochelle worms her way onto Dad's lap. They are such a contrast, my light-skinned, red-headed sister and my dark dad. I sit down at the table across from them.

"Catch me up," he says.

I tell him about school, except for biology, and the Humane Society, and how Hamilton High got to the CIF play-offs in girls' volleyball.

"I wish I could have been here to see the games," he says.

"Miss Lowe says I *have* to sing a solo in choir at our next concert," Rocky says, acting like she hates the idea.

"Of course you should sing a solo—you've got a lot of talent."

Sometimes my dad thinks we're smarter and more talented than we really are, but I guess that's better than having a dad like Danny's, who always thinks the worst.

"How are things in the boyfriend department?" Dad asks, turning to me, suddenly serious.

"Erica's married," Rochelle says.

"Shut up!" I say, socking her on the arm.

"Hey, hey," Dad says. "I just asked a simple question."

"It'll soon be a year for me and Danny," I say.

"Nothing serious, I hope."

"Not serious, just married," Rocky says.

"Rocky!"

"Well, you are married," Rocky says, then totally changes the subject by asking Dad, "Now that you're home can you pick me up after choir practice?"

"I'd like that," Dad says. "Thursdays?"

Rocky gives me a "gotcha" smile that means, I know, if she doesn't need me to pick her up from choir anymore, she can say anything she wants—like she found Danny in my bed that night.

"Want to hear my solo?" Rocky says. She starts singing before Dad has a chance to answer.

I go to my room and change into my Humane Society shirt and a pair of shorts and wait until Rocky sings the last strains of "Oh night divine, Oh night when Christ was born" before I go back to the kitchen. Enough is enough.

Dad looks at me in my work uniform and shakes his head sadly.

"You're growing up so fast, and these past few years . . ."

"I want an electronic keyboard for Christmas," Rochelle says.

Dad laughs. "Don't start with your Christmas lists yet. I just got here."

"I've got to go to work, Dad," I tell him.

"I'll take you, then I can use the car to go get Mom."

"Does she know you're here?"

"No. I didn't call. I'll just walk in to her office and surprise her."

"She told us you'd be home the day before Thanksgiving," I say.

"Yeah, well, I got a chance to get away a week or so early, and it sounded like your mom might need a little help."

Dad looks at me intently, as if he's trying to see inside me.

I remember what Mom had said on her phone call to Dad, after she'd picked me up at the police station—about how hard it was to be mother and father both. Maybe that's why he's home early.

Dad stops at the Humane Society. He touches my shoulder, then runs his hand over my hair, from the top of my head to the middle of my back.

"Your hair is so long, and beautiful," he says. "Remember when you used to only brush the top and underneath was always like a briar patch?"

We both laugh. When I was little, he and Mom would threaten to cut my hair if I couldn't get it tangle free at least once a week.

"I finally took your advice," I smile. "One hundred strokes a night."

"It shows . . . Brains, beauty, muscle—you've got so much going for you, E.J. . . . . Be careful to use it well."

I give him a big hug and get out of the car. I hope he never stops using that English Leather stuff. I also hope Rocky keeps her big mouth shut about Danny being in my bed with me that night. I don't know *what* my dad would say, but it might not be happy talk.

When I get home from work, Mom and Dad and Rocky are sitting at the oak table, playing Scrabble.

"Dad was starving for a Bambino's pizza," Mom says, explaining the pizza box on the table.

"We saved you a piece," Dad says. "I couldn't wait until six to sink my teeth into one of those luscious pieces. I'm sure you'll forgive me if you remember what German pizza tastes like."

"Cardboard," I say, taking the remaining piece—mushrooms, double cheese, black olives—from the box. I put it on a plate, and sit at the table with them.

"Help your sister," Dad says.

I look at the letters in her rack. No wonder she can never figure out a word. She keeps everything in alphabetical order. Right now she has E-I-Q-R-S-T-U.

"Is it your turn?"

"It's *been* her turn for about the last hour," Mom says.

"Long enough for me to redo the locks on all the windows," Dad says. "Have you been hearing strange noises around here at night, Erica? Your mom swears there's a prowler lurking around."

"No," I say, concentrating on rearranging Rocky's letters, putting the Q-U together, and the E-R together.

"Well, it worries me some. Mom's not the type to imagine prowler sounds. I'll work on getting the house more secure before I have to go back to Germany," Dad says.

Suddenly a word pops out at me. I can't believe it!

I put Q-U-I-T down on the board, connect it to an open T and add E-R-S.

Rocky jumps up. "Seven letters! We used all seven letters! How much? How much?"

Dad groans and Mom keeps looking at the board, like maybe there's been some mistake.

Not only do we get fifty points for using all of our letters, the Q is on a triple letter block. All together, QUITTERS is worth one hundred and eighteen points. Rocky is jumping and spinning, which wakes Kitty and she starts running in circles around the house.

"Great play," Mom says.

"I don't want to be a *quitter*," Dad says, "but I'm worn out. How many letters are left in the bag?"

Mom counts. "Only nine."

"I concede to Rocky and the sharp-eyed Erica," he says, standing and stretching. "I've been up for about twenty-three hours, now. I give up."

Mom stands, too, putting her arms around Dad. He hugs her, gently rubbing her back.

"Ummm, I'm glad to be home."

She looks up at him in a way that makes me feel like I'm intruding. They pull away from each other as if they've remembered their audience.

Mom turns to me. "We were talking just before you came home about having a little party," Mom says. "Sort of a combination welcome back to Dad and holiday get-together. We thought maybe you'd like to invite a few friends, too. Maybe April, and Danny, and one or two others, if you'd like."

"I want to invite Jessica and Miss Lowe," Rocky says.

"Your choir teacher?" Mom asks.

"Yeah, I like her."

"Well, we'll see," Mom says, which I know means she doesn't think it's such a great idea.

"It might be awkward for her to come to a party where the only person she knows is one of her students."

"Why?" Rocky asks, turning "why" into a three syllable word.

"We'll talk about it some more tomorrow," Dad says. "I'm beat."

"Goodnight, E.J.," he says, kissing me on the forehead. "Goodnight, Rochelle."

He kisses her, too, then walks down the hall to the bedroom he and my mom share.

I'm so glad he's home. Sometimes I don't even think about how much I miss my dad, until he comes home and I can stop trying *not* to miss him.

"It's time for you to get to your homework, Rochelle," Mom says.

"Can I borrow the car?" I ask Mom.

"Where are you going?"

"I need to look some things up at the library, on the internet," I tell her.

"You'll be back by 9:30?"

"Okay. Or ten?"

She finds her purse and hands me the keys.

"Okay."

The phone rings and I rush to the kitchen to get it, about an arm's reach in front of Rochelle. It's Danny.

"It's Erica's husband. Erica's married," Rocky chants.

"Get a new line, Rocky. This is boring."

I take the phone into my room and shut the door behind me.

Things have been really good between us the past few days—like they were when we first got together.

"Hi, Danny."

"Hi, Pups. How about if I come over later?"

"My dad got home today," I tell him.

"So?"

"So I don't think it's a good idea for you to be climbing through my window. He hears *everything*. He was trained as a Green Beret, so he pays attention to every little thing."

"That was years ago," Danny says. "He's older now."

"He still notices everything. Besides, it's been all I can do to keep Rocky from telling that you were here that night."

There's a long silence, then Danny asks, "Do you still love me?"

"Oh, Danny. I love you more every day. I love you, love you, love you."

"I'm not always sure," he says, sounding sad.

"I *do*, Danny."

"Then why don't I come over, late, and you can *show* me?"

"Not tonight, Danny. I'm really getting scared that we're going to get caught."

"I need so much to feel you close to me," he says.

"Well . . . I've got the car for a little while. I'm going to the library, but . . . "

"Cool. Come pick me up."

"I'm leaving right now. Wait for me in front, okay?"

I tap the phone three times. He taps back four and I hang up. I grab my backpack. Kitty is waiting by the broom closet, where her leash hangs.

"Not tonight," I tell her, scratching her ears. "'Bye, Mom. Thanks."

"Drive carefully," Mom says.

I pull up in front of Alex's house, but Danny's not out there. I honk, and wait, and no Danny. I hope that nosy Alice person from my mom's work isn't anywhere around to see our car here. I walk to the back door and knock. Mrs. Kendall answers. She's wearing stretch pants that are stretched to the limit, and a short blouse that shows her poochy white stomach, like the kind of blouse Hamilton's dress code doesn't allow. It's not exactly a flattering outfit I think, and then immediately feel guilty. Mrs. Kendall's always been nice to me.

"Hi, Erica, come in."

"Is Danny here?"

"DANNY!" she yells at the top of her lungs. "He's around somewhere," she says.

Alex and Joey and some other guys I've seen around but don't know are in the kitchen, drinking beer.

"DANNY!" Alex yells, then smiles at me.

"Turn the goddamned TV down," Alex's mom says, walking into the living room and turning it down. "Are we going out or not?" she yells at some guy I've just noticed who's sitting on the couch in front of the TV watching a hockey game. He yells something at the screen, then turns to her.

"This is just about over, Babe," he says to her.

Danny comes in the back door. "I didn't know you were here," he says.

For the first time, Joey looks up. "Everybody's been yelling their brains out for you. You oughta know."

"You want a beer, Honey?" Mrs. Kendall asks, turning to me.

"No thank you," I say.

"That's *my* beer, Ma," Joey says.

"Yeah? Well, it's *my* house and if I want to offer a guest a beer, I'll do it."

"*Guest?*" Joey spits the word out as if he's offended.

"I'll meet you at the car," I tell Danny.

"I'm ready," he says.

"**I** *hate* going to Alex's," I tell Danny after we get in the car and drive away.

"It's not so bad once you get used to it," Danny says. "It's better than being somewhere like my dad's, where someone's always raggin' on you."

"Joey acts like he hates everyone."

"Yeah, well, things *are* different with Joey there. Alex and his mom are cool, though. Anyway, Alex and I have over $400 saved so we're ready to start looking for our own place."

"$400? How'd you do that?"

"You know that 'don't ask, don't tell' business?"

I shake my head.

"Well, that's the deal with the money. Just be happy I've got it. I've saved some for a big day coming up soon, too," he says, all mysterious.

"I thought you'd forgotten."

"No, Pups. Are you kidding? Our one-year anniversary? I've got plans for this little dark-haired puppy," he says, petting my head.

I pull into the library parking lot and reach for my backpack.

"What's with the library?"

"Come in with me. I've got to find some information for my paper on Kafka," I explain.

Danny pulls me close to him. "Kafka? Is that a disease?"

"No," I laugh. "He was an important writer. Didn't you read that story in senior English, about the guy who turned into a beetle?"

"Can the beetle guy wait?" Danny asks, turning the key in the ignition.

I look at him, torn. The paper is due in three days, and I'm already behind on it, but . . .

Danny kisses me. "Come on," he whispers, "we need a little time together, the two of us."

So I drive out of the library parking lot. We go to a drive-thru for sodas, then on to the deserted hotel where I park in our secret place. Clouds in the sky obscure the moon. I lean close to Danny.

"My parents are having a party a week from Saturday. Will you come?"

"Is your mom still mad at me?"

"No. I told her you had to help Alex's sick uncle—that's why you left in a hurry, without calling her, and why you didn't get back on time."

"Thanks," Danny says.

"So will you come?"

"Sure. I like a party," Danny says with a laugh. "I live in a party right now, at Alex's."

Danny opens one of the little bottles he seems to always have handy and pours it into his soda.

"I think the party my mom and dad are planning is different than Alex's," I say, laughing.

"Yeah. For instance, there'll probably be food and no fights. Ever since Joey got back someone's always getting in a fight."

"Why?"

"Joey's nuts, that's all. Alex tries to keep him in line, but he's worse than ever since he got out of camp."

"What was he in for anyway?"

"Alex never told me. It must have been something sort of bad though because he was in for over two years. That's a long time for a juvenile."

"Juvenile?"

"Yeah. He was only seventeen when he went to camp."

"Did it help him?"

"It helped him get buff. All he did there was lift weights. He was as skinny as Alex when he went in."

"He and Alex seem really different for brothers."

"Lots. You know, Alex may smoke a little bud, but he's a friend to the end. I don't think Joey cares about *anything*. He really gets to me sometimes. Like, the other night, he came into the room where I was sleeping, where I always sleep, and he told me to get up, it was his house and he wanted *that* bed."

"What did you do?"

"Man, I was sound asleep. I just lay there, with him poking and yelling at me. Then Alex's mom came in and got him to leave."

"Maybe you should go back to your dad's."

"No way. Alex and I will get a place together really soon. Alex wants out of there, too. Joey's helped us out some, but you never know what that guy's going to do."

Danny kisses me. "When I get a place, then you and I'll have a place to be, too. No more climbing through windows, or wrestling in the back seat of a car . . . But for now . . ."

Danny gets out of the car and motions for me to do the same. We get into the back seat, where there's more room. When it's over, when I've wiped the tears from Danny's cheeks, when we're holding each other so close I can't tell Danny's heartbeat from my own, I wonder about April's statement—that most girls have sex just to please the boy, and that they regret it later. I don't think that's how it is with us. I know how important it is to Danny, and how comforting, and tonight—maybe tonight I came here more for him than for me. Thoughts crowd in on me, the library work not done, the time, am I late?

I take Danny's hand from where it is resting, fingers in my hair, and bring it eye-level so I can see his watch. 10:15! I sit up straight.

"We've got to go! I said I'd be home by ten."

Danny raises up groggily and straightens and buttons his clothes. I get my clothes straightened, too, then we get in the front seat and I take Danny back to Alex's. Danny takes a little bottle from his jacket pocket and pours it into his empty soda cup.

"Do you ever think you're drinking too much of that stuff?"

"I can quit whenever I want. You want me to cut back? I'll cut back. These are just little bottles, anyway. Don't worry."

CHAPTER

=12=

Two days before the party we start cleaning and cooking. My gramma, my mom's mom, comes to help with food. She's the one I'm named after—Joan.

We'll have beans and tamales, traditional Mexican stuff, and also ham and potato salad. My dad's really into it. It must get boring, in Germany, without us. He eats in the officers' dining room all the time, I guess, so when he gets home he wants to pig out on all his favorite foods.

I'd rather work outside, with Dad and Kitty, than in the kitchen, so I start cultivating the flower beds. Dad's all frustrated though, because the lawnmower stopped working when he was only half-way finished in the front yard.

Gramma comes out onto the porch. She's wearing an apron that comes down past her knees, and her coarse gray hair is pulled back and held in check by a rubber band. She's wearing my old slippers. My old slippers? I stand, stunned, knowing what was in the toes of those slippers.

"Check the gas," she yells to my dad.

Dad gives her a look like, DUH!

"I did that," he says. "Get back in the kitchen."

They both laugh. She's back out in an instant with a big spoonful of potato salad. "Taste this," she says.

He puts it all in his mouth in one big bite. "Yum," he says. "If I wasn't already married to your daughter, I'd ask you to marry me."

She smacks him on the shoulder, playfully, then goes back inside. I follow her, trying not to show I'm in a hurry, pretending I'm interested in what they're doing in the kitchen.

Then I wander nonchalantly back to my bedroom, quietly closing the door behind me. I get down on my hands and knees to check for my slippers. Maybe Gramma has a pair just like mine. No. My slippers are gone. But there, on the floor where they used to be, are the two condoms I have left, and the can of foam. My heart beats fast and I feel all shaky.

Now what? I know for a fact my gramma thinks sex outside of marriage is a giant sin. My face is hot with embarrassment. Maybe I can spend the rest of my life hiding in my closet. But I guess not.

I take the condoms and foam, wrap them carefully in an old T-shirt, and stash the T-shirt in the bottom drawer of my chest, in the back, under a stack of other T-shirts. I've never seen my gramma wearing a T-shirt. It should be a safe hiding place.

I call Danny, dreading talking first to Mrs. Kendall, or Alex, or worst of all, Joey, but today Danny's the one who answers.

"Danny?"

"What's up, Pups?"

"Something terrible. My gramma's walking around, wearing my *slippers*."

"So?"

"So. You know. My slippers! The ones I keep the condoms and foam hidden in. Lots of times when she's here she borrows my shoes, but those were *way* in the back. What'll I do?"

"Hey, don't get all stressed out. She probably doesn't even know what that stuff is," Danny says. "Besides, shouldn't she be glad you're responsible?"

"But Danny! She's super religious! I'm scared. What if she tells my parents?"

"Listen, why don't you come over here for awhile. Relax."

"I can't. I'm supposed to be helping with the party. But maybe you could come over here? If you helped out you might get back on my mom's good side."

"Yeah, I guess."

"Do they have a lawnmower over there we could borrow? Ours

quit working."

"Yeah, maybe. Alex is having trouble with his car, though. Can you come get me?"

"Okay," I say. "Check about the lawnmower, would you? I know Dad'll let me use the car if it includes coming back with a lawnmower."

I wait for awhile for Danny to check the garage. What is my gramma thinking about me right now? I'm so embarrassed!

"No power mower, but there's an old push mower. Why don't I bring it over? I'll mow the lawn for your dad."

Danny can be so sweet sometimes.

I walk through the kitchen, afraid to look at my gramma, wondering if she is really watching me from the corner of her eye, or if I am imagining things. I go out the back door and walk around to where my dad is still fiddling with the lawnmower.

"Can I borrow the car and go get Danny? He's got a push mower he can bring over."

"Sure," Dad says. "But I hate push mowers."

"Danny says he'll mow the lawn for you."

Dad looks up, wiping the sweat from his forehead with the back of his hand. He reaches for the keys and tosses them to me.

"C'mon, Kitty," I say. "Let's go get Danny."

She does her usual fast wide circle, twice, and then, as soon as I open the door, she bounds into the back seat, smiling. I swear she's smiling.

Alex and his brother, Joey, and Danny are in the driveway, standing by Alex's car, fiddling around with something under the hood. Kitty runs up to Danny, who reaches down to pet her. Joey backs away, a screwdriver poised in his hand.

"She won't hurt you," Alex says.

"Hi," Joey says, glancing my way for just an instant, then looking back at Kitty. I've never seen anyone be afraid of Kitty before. Alex calls to her and scratches her behind her ears.

"Pet her, man. She's cool," Alex says, but Joey keeps his

distance.

"Here, Kitty," Danny calls, and she follows him down the driveway and into the garage.

"Gina broke up with me," Alex says.

"Why?" I ask, unable to tell whether Alex even cares or not.

"Said I was acting like a loser," Alex laughs. "I told her it wasn't an act."

"Girls are a pain in the ass, anyway," Joey says, looking at me. "They get all lovey-dovey over you and then they think they own you."

"We'd been together over a year," Alex says, ignoring his brother's remarks.

"Maybe she'll change her mind," I say.

Alex looks down and shakes his head. I see now that he does care.

"Forget the bitch," Joey says.

I walk back toward the garage, sick of Joey's remarks.

Danny comes out, pushing the lawnmower, with Kitty prancing behind him, carrying an old baseball like it's a great treasure. She drops the ball at Joey's feet, trying to make friends, I guess. Joey picks it up and throws it, hard.

"Kitty!" I scream, as she runs full speed down the driveway and into the street, into the path of an oncoming car. I stand frozen, as brakes screech and the car swerves. Then I see Kitty, the ball in her mouth, trot back across the street, wagging her tail. Danny, Alex and I all exhale as in one relieved breath.

Joey laughs. "Stupid dog," he says.

"You're the one who's stupid," I say, leading Kitty to the car and getting in.

Danny puts the lawnmower in the trunk and we leave.

"What a total butthole," I say, feeling all shaky inside over what almost happened.

"He just doesn't know anything about dogs," Danny says.

"Any butthole in the world knows not to throw a ball out into the middle of a street for a dog to chase after it."

Danny leans over and kisses my cheek and nuzzles my neck.

"What'd your gramma say? Anything?"

"No. I've sort of avoided her since I saw she was wearing my slippers."

"She doesn't even know about that stuff," Danny says. "She's old."

"I don't think she's *that* old."

"Well, even if she knows, I bet she'll just keep it to herself."

"I hope so, but I feel really funny about it."

I park our car out front because I know Dad will want to hose down the driveway when we're all finished working in the yard. He straightens up from where he's been working in the front flower bed.

"Hey, Danny," he says, wiping his hand on his jeans as he walks toward us.

"You look thinner than the last time I saw you," Dad says, extending his hand. "Life treating you okay?"

"Fine," Danny says with a smile, shaking Dad's hand.

"How's school coming?"

I hate when my dad does that stuff. He knows Danny's not in school right now because he's already asked me about it. Actually, he's already lectured me about Danny not being in school. I hope he's not going to start lecturing Danny.

"I'm sort of on a break from school right now," Danny says. "I'll start up again in September."

"Don't let it go," Dad says.

"Erica, would you come in for a minute?" Gramma calls to me from the front window.

Suddenly my mouth is dry and my palms are all sweaty. I go inside, to the kitchen where she and Mom and Rocky are making enchiladas.

Gramma looks at me and I look away. She hands me a five dollar bill.

"I forgot cilantro and chipotle chiles. Will you go to that Mexican market over on Hill Street and pick some up? And get some fresh tortillas for our lunch, too."

"Sure," I say, meeting her eyes for a moment. I can't tell what she's thinking. I hope it's all related to food.

At lunchtime everybody takes a still-warm tortilla, or two or three, from the package sitting on the kitchen counter, and spoons beans, rice, salsa and cheese into them. Everybody but me helps themselves to the chorizo Gramma has just fried. I haven't eaten any little piggies since I decided they had a right to live, too.

We take our food outside, on the patio.

"I can't believe it's almost December and we're out here in our shirtsleeves," Dad says.

"California has some definite advantages over Germany, doesn't it?" Mom smiles at Dad.

"Definite," he says, leaning over and kissing her.

Rocky scoots her chair between where Danny and I are sitting.

"Will you come to my Christmas concert?" she asks him, leaning her head against his shoulder. "I'm singing a solo."

"Hey, Rocks, I know about your solo. Remember? You sang it for me."

"But will you come to my concert?"

"I wouldn't miss it. When?"

"The Sunday before Christmas."

Danny reaches into his shirt pocket, pulls out an imaginary date book, and pretends to be flipping the pages.

"Yep, that date's open. I'll pencil you in," he says, acting like he's writing something.

We all laugh, especially Rocky and my gramma. But then, I think she ends up looking at Danny in a kind of funny way. This whole thing is making me paranoid.

Late in the evening, after all of the work is done and things are cleaned up, we rent that movie, "Moonstruck." My mom *loves* that movie, like Nicolas Cage is the man of her dreams or something. But it's pretty funny. My mom and Danny laugh at all the same places, and I can tell she's not mad at him anymore. And my dad has thanked Danny about a thousand times for bringing over the lawn mower and then mowing the lawn. I really like it when everyone I love gets along together.

After "Moonstruck" my dad puts a new CD on the stereo.

"I got this for you," he says to Mom. He has this big grin on his face that makes him look about ten years younger.

"Do you remember, do you recall . . . ," the strains of an old song start . . . "I want to tell you . . ."

They both start singing when it gets to the part about the "sea of love."

"Remember this?" Dad says, taking Mom by the hand and leading her to the middle of the floor.

They put their arms around each other and sort of dance/sway together.

"They don't make music like this anymore," Dad says to us, then turns back to Mom and kisses the top of her head.

"I wanna dance," Rochelle says, pushing between them. They make room for her and dance as a threesome until the end of the song.

When we've heard enough of The Honey Drippers, I take Danny home, with a stop at our secret place first.

"You've got such a great family," Danny says. "That's how we're going to be when we're married and have kids."

I never know what to say when Danny starts talking about getting married, it all seems so far away. I know I want to be with him my whole life, but I always think about marriage like something in the way distant future, after college and after I'm a vet, which is like about a million years away.

"Your dad was trying to talk me into joining the army," Danny says.

"Really?"

"Yeah. He said if I got my G.E.D. and scored high on the Armed Services test I could probably get a good deal."

"So?"

"Nah. I'm not ready for boot camp. Besides, things are going pretty good for me right now," he says, kissing me.

I lean my head on his shoulder, remembering how close we came to breaking up just a few weeks ago, and thinking how good things have been between us since then.

When I get back home, about one o'clock in the morning, my mom and dad are still up. The house is decorated for tomorrow's party, but they don't look happy. They're in the family room, the place they watch TV, but the TV is not on.

"I've got to be at work at nine tomorrow morning," I say. "'Night."

"Sit down," Dad says, in the voice I've heard him use with lower ranking army personnel who've not been doing their jobs right. I sit, my heart pounding.

"Why do you keep condoms and foam in your closet?" Dad asks.

"And worse!" Mom says. "What do you mean by letting Danny sneak into *our* house at night? And *then* acting like I'm crazy, hearing things in the dark?"

"I never said you were crazy," I say.

"Well, you might as well have!"

"Well, I *didn't!*"

"What you *didn't* say is not the point," Dad yells. "The point is, you've been very sneaky—basically dishonest—and it all has to do with Danny."

I don't know what to say. Apparently Gramma and Rocky found a lot to talk about while I was gone.

As if he's just read my mind, Dad says, "Don't go blaming your grandmother or your sister, either. *You're* the one who's been misbehaving."

After a long silence Mom says, "We were talking after you left tonight, saying what a sweet boy Danny is, and maybe he's past the hard part with his mom's death and all, he seemed so comfortable here today, and we're happy for you, that you have a nice boyfriend, and Rocky announces to us that he's not just your boyfriend, he's your husband. Well, you know, she always says that and we never pay any attention, but Gramma took it seriously, said how that explained the birth control things she found in your closet."

Mom starts to cry, and Daddy puts his arm around her.

"Then Rocky says she *knows* you're married because Danny sleeps in your bed," Dad says. He looks at me like he doesn't even know me, and suddenly I understand how Gregor Samsa must have felt when his family saw that he'd turned into a beetle.

"But, why are you so mad at me? You've always warned me not ever to have unprotected sex!"

"Oh, did I forget to say don't be a sneak?" Mom says.

"I'm sure! Did you expect me to come running to you to tell you Danny and I were thinking about having sex? Should I have asked you to sign a parent permission slip?"

"Don't you get sarcastic with me, Erica! You know damned well what I'm talking about. When I was so worried about prowlers, did it ever occur to you to say that Danny'd been here?"

Dad draws a deep breath and says quietly, "Erica, look at me."

I raise my eyes and look at him. "We love you, Erica. We're just trying to understand what's going on here. We've always trusted you to be honest with us and . . ."

"I love Danny, okay? Is there anything wrong with that?"

"Oh, E.J.," Dad sighs. "Of course there's nothing wrong with loving someone, unless it's turning you into someone you don't want to be—someone who's sneaky, or who gets in trouble with the police, or who no longer does well in school."

I don't know what else to say and I guess they don't either. We just sit there. Finally Dad says, "Let's call it a night."

I walk through the kitchen, picking up the cordless phone on my way. Dad follows me and gently takes the phone from my hand and puts it back on the receiver.

"Think about this on your own tonight. Morning will be soon enough to call Danny, or April, or whoever it is you want to hash things over with."

I lie awake for a long time. It's a strange feeling, knowing my parents are hurt and disappointed in me. They've been mad at me plenty of times before, like for not doing my chores, or for picking on Rocky, but this feels different, like there's a wedge between us.

Kitty is stretched out, snoring, at the end of my bed. I give her a nudge with my foot to wake her, and she slowly inches her way up next to me. I pet her silky head, remembering the screech of brakes and the really close call she had earlier today.

"You've got to be careful," I tell her. "You almost got yourself killed just by playing with that jerk, Joey. You can't trust everyone, you know?"

Kitty sidles up closer to me and sighs a long sigh, as if to say I know what you mean. I think how awful it would have been if she'd been hit by that car.

13

Ever since our big argument over Danny, I've felt awkward with my parents. On the night of their party, I stay just long enough to say hello to people, then go to April's to spend the night. The first thing we do when I get there is prepare to munch out.

April and I cover a huge batch of tortilla chips with grated cheese and zap them in the microwave, then smother them in salsa. We get sodas, and napkins, and take everything into her room, where she has her own giant TV complete with a laserdisc set-up.

I borrow a pair of sweatpants and a T-shirt from April's vast supply, and we get comfortable. April puts on last year's Hamilton High softball team sweatshirt.

"Will you go out for softball again when it starts up second semester?" I ask.

"Of course. Won't you?"

"Of course," I say.

We watch April's favorite movie of all time, "Racing With the Moon." April is totally in love with Sean Penn.

"For him I'd throw away my born-again virgin chastity belt," she says, making us both laugh.

"He's too old for you."

"Look at him!" she tells me.

"This movie is not exactly a recent release."

"You're just jealous because he's not your guy."

"He's not *your* guy either."

"He could be," she says, all serious, which makes me laugh even harder.

We talk for a long time about the movie. The scene where Nicolas Cage's girlfriend goes for an illegal abortion is so sad.

"That's how it was in the old days, though," April says. "Sometimes girls *died* because they'd get infections from having abortions that weren't done right—Nicolas Cage is such a jerk," she adds.

"I know. Here's this girl going through hell because he got her pregnant, and he can't think about anyone but himself."

"Guys are like that," April says.

"Not all of them," I tell her, feeling somehow as if I have to defend Danny, even though she hasn't said a word about him.

April gives me a look, like maybe she *wants* to say more, but instead she removes the "Racing with the Moon" disc and inserts "Fast Times at Ridgemont High." I go to the kitchen for sodas.

April's mom is standing at the kitchen counter with a big bowl of vanilla ice cream topped with chocolate chips. She is maxed out in the weight department, but I like her a lot.

"Oh, hi, Erica . . . Want some?" she says, holding the bowl out for me to take a look.

"No thanks. April and I have nachos."

She asks me the usual adult questions, how's school, how're my mom and dad, what are my plans after graduation. I give the usual kid answers, fine and college, and then go back to April's room.

"I love this part," she says, laughing.

It's the part where Sean Penn has a pizza delivered to his history classroom.

"Wouldn't old Blakely poop his pants if someone had pizza delivered to *his* history class?"

"Even gum chewing gives Blakely a nervous breakdown," I say.

We watch the rest of the movie, finishing the nachos and sodas.

"I'm so full I could barf," April says.

I climb into the extra bed and snuggle under the covers. It must be about three in the morning. April turns out the light and gets into her bed.

"I'm glad you came over tonight."

"Me, too. I haven't laughed this much in a long time," I say, drifting somewhere between being awake and asleep.

"We should do this more often, like we always used to do, before you got all tied up with Danny Lara."

"I'm not exactly tied up."

"Whatever," she says.

It's dark in here and I can't see April's face, but she sounds angry to me. That's how she usually sounds when the subject of Danny comes up. She used to like Danny, but not lately. I don't know why—jealous maybe.

"Sean Penn was such a burnout in 'Fast Times'," I say. Anything to change the subject.

"At least he wasn't selling drugs to junior high kids," she says.

"What do you mean?"

"You know. Sean Penn was only using it, he wasn't selling it."

"So?"

"So all I'm saying is you can't complain about Sean Penn when you hang around with Danny Lara."

My eyes are wide open now and my head is spinning. What does April mean? And why don't I want to know?

"Danny doesn't even use that stuff anymore," I tell her.

"Right, just like he doesn't drink anymore?"

"No. I know he still drinks, sometimes too much. But he's working on it."

"Yeah. Like my mom is working on a size eight figure. Get a clue."

I hear April turn over in her bed and I know that means she's ready for sleep. In no time I hear her deeper, steady breathing, but now I'm wide awake. I think about the baggies of marijuana, and the $400 Danny says he has saved, and how he always seems to have money these days.

Maybe I shouldn't settle for his "don't ask, don't tell" answers. Whatever maybes there are, I know one thing for certain. I'll do my best to help Danny get back to being the kind of guy he was in the picture that sits on my desk at home. I love him and he loves me. That's what matters.

It's the rhythm of words, over and over, that finally puts me to sleep—"I love him, he loves me. That's what matters, don't you see"—to the tune of the Barney song.

Thursday afternoon I spend about an hour trying to write just the right thing on the card I bought Danny for our anniversary. I'm almost finished when he calls.

"Happy anniversary," he says. "Can you believe it's a year? So much has happened."

"I know. Good and bad."

"But you've been all good," he says. "Alex is letting me borrow his car for tonight. I'll come get you about seven?"

"Okay. I bought something special for you," I tell him.

"I bought something special for you, too."

We talk for awhile, then Danny says, "I'll just honk for you. Be ready. Okay?"

"Oh, no. My parents would go nuts. You've got to come to the door, like that gentleman kind of stuff. Don't make things worse by honking."

"But Pups . . ."

"No, Danny. I mean it. You haven't been inside my house since Gramma and Rocky told on us. My dad says you're cowardly."

There's a long pause. "I *am* cowardly," he says.

"Well, don't honk. Ring the doorbell like you always used to do," I say.

"Okay. Listen. I want this to be special for us tonight. I know sometimes I'm not the best boyfriend in the world. But I want to be."

"You're the best boyfriend for me," I tell him. I tap three times and he taps four, and we hang up.

At seven o'clock sharp, Danny rings the doorbell. Rocky runs to answer it.

"Hey, Rocks," he says, laughing.

She throws her arms around him like he's *her* boyfriend, not mine.

He looks so good. Sometimes I still can hardly believe that he's really my boyfriend. My dad comes into the room and they shake hands, polite, but not exactly friendly.

"Have a seat," Dad says, motioning toward the couch.

"We probably should get going," Danny says to me. "I have dinner reservations."

I pick up the package I wrapped earlier, and the card that took me all afternoon to write, and give my dad a peck on the cheek.

"'Bye, Rocky," I say, and walk out the front door with Danny.

"Everything seems all fine at your house. I don't know why you were so worried."

"I guess everything's normal on the surface. But sometimes I feel one of my parents just looking at me, like you might look at someone with a handicap, carefully, out of the corner of your eye. Things still feel kind of weird to me."

We get in the car. "I've never seen this car so clean."

"I've worked on it all day. I told Alex I'd detail it for him. He lets me use it pretty often—carpets, trunk, everything is spotless."

Shinto's is one of the best restaurants in the San Gabriel Valley. It was even written up in a fancy restaurant guide. The waiters are more dressed up than we are, and we're as dressed up as we've ever been, except for last year's prom.

Danny orders a soda for each of us. The waiter brings it and then takes our dinner order. I only order a dinner salad because everything is so expensive. But Danny orders a Porterhouse steak, which is practically the most expensive thing on the menu.

"Have more than a salad," he urges me. "I can afford it."

But I'm embarrassed to call the waiter back, so I stick with my order.

Danny glances around to be sure no one is paying attention, then takes a little Jack Daniels bottle from his pants pocket and empties half of it into his soda.

"Want some?" he asks.

I shake my head no.

"Not even for this special occasion?"

"No, thanks," I say, feeling disappointed that he's even asked—disappointed that he's brought whiskey with him for our celebration—like being with me isn't enough.

Danny pours the rest of the bottle into his soda and takes a long drink.

"I don't get why we need two forks and two spoons," Danny says.

"I think it's kind of a show-off thing," I say.

"We're lucky to find *one* fork at Alex's," he says with a laugh. "And that fork usually sits on the table all week long."

The waiter brings bread that's still warm, with a big hunk of butter, not butter divided into equal little pats on cardboard squares, like I'm used to seeing in the restaurants my parents sometimes take us on special occasions.

"Can you believe we're here?" Danny says, gesturing with his eyes around the room.

There are tablecloths on the tables, and cloth napkins, and each table has a real flower in a vase. The hardwood floors are highly polished, and, in the next room, a man in a tuxedo is playing music on a grand piano. We hold hands under the table and talk about all we've been through together, and how we always will be together, no matter what.

"I've decided, it's time for me to stop messing around. I'll take the high school equivalency test and then start community college in September. I want you to be proud of me, Pups."

"Are you thinking of environmental studies?" I ask, knowing that was his plan last year, when he was applying to colleges, before everything fell apart.

"Maybe business," he says. "I think I have a talent for business."

"Really?"

The waiter brings our dinners and Danny orders another soda, which he spikes with another little whiskey bottle.

"And this, you don't have to worry. I'm only going to use it for special occasions, not every day anymore."

When it is time to pay, I'm surprised to see how much money Danny takes from his pocket. He counts it out carefully, then figures out a tip.

"Twice as much as the tax is what Alex's mom told me," Danny explains. First he tries figuring it out in his head. Then he asks, a little too loudly, to borrow a pencil from a passing waiter. He writes on the check, and I see that he's having trouble multiplying by two. I guess it's the whiskey. He puts down enough tip money to eat for a whole month at the Golden Arches, and we leave.

We go to our secret place and park. Danny kisses me, long, then reaches into the glove compartment for another little Jack Daniels bottle and downs it. He sits, staring out the windshield at I don't know what. Then he says, "Sometimes, when you're not around, I feel like I'm floating in space. I need you so much, Pups," he says.

"I'll always be there for you, Danny. You know that," I say, kissing him, holding him close.

"I've got something for you," he says.

"Let me give you yours, first."

I hand Danny the gift that took most of my two paychecks to buy. He opens it quickly.

"Wow. A walkman!"

"I know you miss your stereo, and you're always complaining about the music at Alex's house, so now you can always have your own—here, listen to it. It's already got a tape in it."

Danny puts on the headphones, presses play, and leans his head back, eyes closed. After a minute or so I tap him on the shoulder. He turns it off and takes off the headphones. His eyes are all shiny.

"It's a really good one," I say. "Not one of those cheap kinds that sounds all distorted."

"I love you, Pups," he says. "You're the best thing that's ever happened to me."

He reaches past me, into the glove compartment. I'm afraid it's for another Jack Daniels, but instead he pulls out a small package and hands it to me. Just as I'm starting to open it, I'm startled by headlights turning onto the road where we've never seen anyone else before.

"Shit!" Danny says.

"What?"

"The cops."

We watch as the car drives slowly past where we're sitting and parks not more than fifty feet from us, facing the road. Danny starts the engine and drives slowly out toward the street.

"Fuckin' pigs!"

I turn and look back and see that the police car is following us. I think about the little bottles of whiskey. God.

On the street, Danny turns left, then makes the first right he can. They follow. Please, please don't flash your red lights, I urge, trying to send a psychic message back to the police. Please, please don't let me get arrested again. Don't make my parents come get me. My hands are sweaty and my heart is pounding. Why? I haven't done anything wrong. I look over at Danny. He seems sober now, but I don't know if he could pass one of those line-walking, nose-touching sobriety tests or not.

We keep driving, under the speed limit, toward my house.

"Why don't those bastards work on making the streets safe instead of harassing citizens?" Danny says.

"Why don't they either pull us over or leave us alone?" I ask.

"We should have used your parents' car tonight."

"Why?"

"Then we wouldn't have had to put up with this," Danny says, glancing in the rear-view mirror.

"What difference would that have made?"

"Alex's car. They're always after Alex, just because he's Joey's brother. They follow him all around. They'll never get anything on him, though. Alex is smart. It may not seem like it, but he is."

"But why would they be like that?"

"Once they get it in for you, they can't leave you alone."

"It doesn't make sense," I say.

"Yeah, well there's a lot that might not make sense to you that I know about," Danny says.

He seems all tight and closed now, as he turns into my driveway. The cops pull up to the curb across the street and wait, lights on, engine running.

"I better take Alex's car home and get these pigs off my back," Danny says, glancing again at the car across the street.

I don't say anything about the package which still sits unopened on my lap, and neither does Danny. It hasn't exactly been the perfect anniversary celebration I'd anticipated. I put the box on the dashboard when I get out of the car. Danny is so preoccupied he doesn't even notice.

"'Night, Pups," he says.

I barely get the car door closed before he's backing out the driveway.

In my room I pick up the picture of us at last year's Winter Fantasy. Danny's eyes were bright and clear, his face open and unguarded. The corsage I was wearing was an unusual kind of flower that Danny's mother had helped him choose. I remember feeling so special just being with Danny Lara, who was popular and handsome, and who loved me.

That night Mark, a football player, had started hitting on me while I was talking to April. When Danny got back from the restroom, he stood next to me. That's all he did, and Mark got all red in the face and left. Even if Danny wasn't a jock, he had a lot of respect. Kids turned to his column first when the *Hamilton Herald* came out, because he always had something important to say, and it was often funny. I wonder if he'll ever get back to anything like that? Tonight was the first time I'd ever heard him say anything about having a talent for business. What did that mean?

14

"**Y**ou were home a little early last night," is the first thing my dad says to me when I go to breakfast. "How was your dinner?"

"Nice," I say.

I pour a glass of orange juice and put some bread in the toaster.

"I see you had a police escort. What was that about?"

My dad, the Green Beret. Of course he would notice.

"It was so weird," I say, both wanting and not wanting to tell him about it. Wanting to tell wins out.

"We were parked back by that old hotel, just talking," I say.

"Right," Dad says, sarcastic.

"We were just *talking*," I insist.

"Sure," Dad says. "Tell me about the police."

"They parked near us and just sat and watched."

"They didn't get out of the car, or ask you to get out of the car?"

"No. They just sat. So we left, and they followed us here."

"They didn't ever pull you over?"

I shake my head no.

"They're harassing Alex," I say, repeating what Danny told me. "They follow his car all the time—isn't there some law against that, Dad?"

Dad pours himself another cup of coffee and stirs it thoughtfully.

"I doubt that the police are the ones breaking the law here," he says.

"We weren't doing anything wrong," I say.

"There's a reason the police are watching Alex's car. Those boys are into something they shouldn't be. Where did Danny get enough money to take you to Shinto's when he doesn't even have a job?"

"I don't know. He saved it, I guess."

"Saved it from what?"

Now I'm sorry I told Dad anything. It's just another excuse for him to think the worst of Danny.

"Erica, Danny's not the same young man he was when you first got together with him. He's changed, and not for the better."

I finish my orange juice and put my glass in the dishwasher.

"Sweetheart, I know he's been through a hard time with the death of his mother, but that's no excuse for him to continue to float aimlessly along. It's time for him to find a purpose . . ."

"Whatever," I say, relieved to hear April's car pull into the driveway to take me to school.

Ms. Lee calls me up to her desk at the end of the period.

"I'm concerned about you, Erica. You've missed three assignments recently. That's not like you."

"I'm making them up."

"You know, your grade will be lowered because they're late."

"I know."

"Is everything all right at home?"

"Fine," I say.

"Ms. Costanza tells me you've fallen back a bit in biology, too."

I hate how teachers gossip. Don't they have anything better to do than sit around talking about how their students are messing up?

"Are you keeping up with the reading?" she asks.

"I've finished 'Metamorphosis.' It was good."

"Highly symbolic," she says. "Organisms metamorphose in many ways. I hope you're not in the process of metamorphosing into a poor student."

She says it as a joke, but on the bus, on my way to work, I think about changes—how I don't feel as lighthearted as I once did, and how things feel strained between me and my parents, and even at times with April, who I've been totally close to for years. I determine not to let myself get caught in a metamorphosis that would totally separate me from my family and friends. I definitely do not want to end up like poor Gregor.

"**H**ey, Beauty. Today is bath day," I tell my patient, taking her from the cage and into what the staff jokingly calls "the spa."

I fill the tub with warm water, put on a vinyl apron, and lift Beauty into her bath. As soon as I wet her down she starts trembling.

"It's okay. It's okay. You're going to feel so much better . . . " I carry on a running monologue of what I hope is soothing patter, while I soap and rinse, soap and rinse, careful to shield her eyes.

After her bath, I put her on the high metal table and secure her with a short leash. I towel dry her first, then use a blow dryer. When she is reasonably dry I take her out to a larger cage in the kennel, where it's sunny, and brush her. Her black hair shines in the sunlight, and the white markings are truly white for the first time since I've known her. The patches on her coat are beginning to fill in and her ears are perky now, as if there might be something worth listening for.

"You're still pretty skinny, though," I tell her.

When I'm finished grooming her I walk her upstairs to where Sinclair is working in his office.

"Oh, my," he says, clapping his hands. "I just *love* your make-over, girl." He leans down and pets her. She wags her tail vigorously. "We should have before and after pictures," he tells me.

"HELLO. HELLO. HELLO." The parrot screeches from its cage by the door. Beauty stands on her hind legs, trying to get a look at the bird.

"I have a big favor to ask you," Sinclair says.

"What?"

"You know how my parents never invite me to their holiday gatherings?"

I nod.

"Well, they've invited me to come to their Christmas Eve party. It's kind of a big step for them, to claim me in front of their friends."

"You should go."

"Right. That's where you come in. I need someone to cover the office until six."

"Six? On Christmas Eve?"

Sinclair just sits petting Beauty, looking at me.

Our family tradition is to wrap packages all that day, and decorate the house, while a big pot of albóndigas soup simmers on the stove. We eat soup and French bread in the afternoon. Dad always says that proves we are eclectic. Then we go buy a tree and haul it home, trim it and put the packages around. I'll miss a lot of that if I have to work until six.

"I know it's a lot to ask . . . "

I remember the sadness I felt coming from Sinclair, when he first told me of how he never saw his family for holidays.

"I can work for you," I say.

"Thanks, Erica."

"No problem."

I take Beauty back downstairs and set her up in an outside pen, where there's room for her to walk around. I get a clean padded mat and put it under the sheltered area. This is a state-of-the-art facility, with individual kennels that allow for sun, shade, and shelter from the rain. There is no artificial light either in the kennels or in the cat shelter.

"You've got a new house," I tell Beauty.

I move her identification card from the infirmary to the new spot, then go back to the infirmary to begin prepping animals for surgery. We're doing three dogs and four cats today. I help Morris, one of the health technicians, give the animals pre-anesthetics, then we shave and scrub each of them.

Dr. Franz comes to tell us she'll take the first surgery at four. April thinks it's gross to have a job where ovaries and testicles get sent off to a rendering service and turned into fertilizer. What I know, though, is that for every set of reproductive organs removed, there are lots fewer animals whose remains end up strewn around flowers.

A few days after our anniversary, Danny catches up to me at school, when I'm on my way to biology.

"Let's take a break, Pups."

I stop. "Now?"

"Yeah. Now's the best time," Danny smiles.

"I've got to go to biology."

"You're hardly ever absent," Danny says. "Once won't hurt."

"No. Really. I can't afford to mess up any more, not even a little."

"Well. Meet me at lunch then, at the park," he says. "I have something for you."

"Okay."

He gives me a quick kiss and is gone.

At lunchtime, at the park, Danny hands me the package I didn't open the other night.

"You left this in the car," he says, smiling the smile I love.

"I didn't know if I should take it or not," I say. "You were all quiet."

"I was mad! Not at you, but at the cops. They had no right to follow us around like that. If I was a rich white kid, they wouldn't think of harassing me like that. But because I'm just a poor Mexican whose dad doesn't believe in backing him up, they think they can do whatever they want."

"It wasn't exactly Rodney King," I say.

"Both cops were Mexican, too," he says, ignoring my Rodney King remark. "They're the worst kind, going against their own people."

I sort of want to argue with Danny. A week or so ago he was complaining because it's mostly white guys who get to be police and they take all of their prejudices out on everybody else, and now he's unhappy with the Mexican cops. I glance over at him and see that dark, closed look on his face, and decide not to point out his contradictions.

"Here, Pups, open this," he says, his mood lifting as quickly as it fell.

I take the package from him and sit on a bench, under a tree. I open it carefully, without seeming to be in a hurry, the way my mother taught me when I was only five or six. Resting on white tissue paper is a large, silver barrette, with a simple, engraved design around the edges.

"It's beautiful," I tell Danny.

"Look at the back."

I turn the barrette over and open the clasp. There, on the back, is engraved, "First Anniversary, My love forever, Danny."

"Oh, Danny, I love it. I love you."

He kisses me. "I know," he says.

"Put it on."

I get my brush from my backpack and brush my hair, then fasten the barrette over a section, pulling it back and away from my face.

"It *is* beautiful," Danny says, straightening it a bit, running his fingers through my hair.

"There's something else," he says, pointing to a tiny, neatly wrapped package, no more than one inch square.

"I didn't even notice this," I say, taking it from the box and unwrapping it carefully.

It's a thin, gold ring, with a small stone in the middle.

"Look, it's a real diamond. Not big, but real," he smiles, slipping the ring onto my ring finger, left hand.

"It's so pretty," I say, watching the stone reflect cloud-filtered sunlight.

Danny jiggles the ring a bit. "Is it too big?" he asks.

I move it from my left hand to my right.

"This is a better fit," I say.

"But I got it for your left hand."

"We're not really engaged, though."

"No, but we will be."

"Danny . . . I'm not sure . . . I love you and I know I'll always love you, but . . ."

"But what?"

"But, neither of us is ready to think about marriage . . ."

"I am," he says, his mouth pulling down the way it does when he's hurt.

"But Danny, we've both got school to . . ."

"Look. I'm making money, I don't have to borrow from you anymore. I don't really need school."

"That's another thing. I don't even know *how* you're making money, but I've got an idea it may not be legal."

"Just trust me, Pups."

"Do you trust *me*, keeping these big mysterious, don't ask, don't tell secrets?"

Danny looks away, sighing, then looks back at me.

"Just let me get it made smaller for you. It doesn't have to mean we're engaged."

"But that's what people will think it means . . . let me wear it on my right hand for now, so I can show April, and Rocky. Rocky'll be so jealous," I say.

"Okay. But will you at least think about it?"

I nod.

"I'm sorry you didn't get to open it on our actual anniversary."

"Really, Danny, policemen following us. I don't like it. And I'm afraid maybe there's a reason."

"Fuckin' pigs . . ." Danny says, suddenly angry.

I think of the old Danny, before his mom died, and wish again that my mellow Danny would return.

"Can you come over Christmas Eve and help us trim the tree?" I ask, wanting to move to a safe subject. "And Christmas Day, for dinner?"

"Are you sure it's okay? Lately I think your parents don't like me so much."

"Lately they're upset with me, too. But they said they'd like to have you join us. April's coming over too. It'll be fun. It's always fun at our house on Christmas Eve."

"Things are so different for me now, from last Christmas," Danny says.

"I know," I say, remembering how his mom had decorated the house, and how she and Danny put up thousands of lights—enough lights that people went out of their way to drive their little kids past the Laras' house. This season probably all they'll see when they drive by is a yard that's all overgrown and a For Sale sign in front.

We sit on the swings, swaying gently in parallel motion. Two moms, each with a little boy in tow, walk to a picnic table near the slides and set out lunch. It is cloudy, but not cold, not like December where it snows. The boys, five years old maybe, race to the tallest slide and climb the ladder, one after the other.

"Look, Mom! Look!" the first one yells.

Both mothers turn and look up, smiling, at their sons.

Our swings are barely moving now, as Danny and I silently watch the scene before us, the clouds, the trees, the familiar park, the little boys and their moms.

══ 15 ══

Christmas Eve, when I walk out to the parking lot to meet Mom, April is waiting for me instead. She has Rocky and Kitty in the car with her and they're all full of Christmas spirit—even Kitty it seems, who barks and wags her tail as the other two sing "Deck the halls with boughs of holly. . ." at the top of their lungs.

At least it's not "Oh Holy Night." Really, that used to be one of my favorite Christmas songs, but after about the billionth time of hearing Rocky practice it, I hope I never have to hear it again. I have to admit hers was probably the best solo at the concert the other night, though. The rest of the kids should have practiced as much as she did.

I get in the back seat, next to Kitty.

"We've waited for you to get off work before we trim the tree," Rocky says.

"Tell the truth, Rocks," April says. "You didn't *want* to wait for your hardworking sister, did you?"

"Well, I just wanted to put a few decorations on," Rocky whines.

"Yeah? Didn't I hear you complaining about why you all had to wait for *Erica* when she's hardly ever home anymore?"

"You don't know everything, April!" Rochelle says.

They make me laugh, the way they argue just like *they're* sisters sometimes.

April turns to look at me. "Your dad said trimming the tree

without you wouldn't seem like Christmas and Rocky would have to put her underdeveloped skill of patience to work."

"April! Look where you're going!"

April swerves back into her own lane, barely missing a car to our right.

"Oh, yeah," she says. "I still forget I'm driving sometimes."

"Stupid!" Rocky says.

"Hey. You don't like it, you can just get out, you little twit," April says, slowing down and pulling over to the curb.

"I like it," Rocky says.

April starts up again.

I'm still thinking about what April said earlier—how my dad said it wouldn't be Christmas if I wasn't there to trim the tree. My throat gets all tight—like I could cry. Dad and I always used to joke around, and he'd take me wherever he went. Sometimes we'd cook stuff together.

My dad loves pies and he knows how to make really good crusts. I'd cut up apples while he'd make a crust. He'd always make plenty, so we could make cinnamon roll-up things with the leftover dough. But none of that has been happening since he found out Danny'd been sneaking in through my window.

Ever since our big argument, things have seemed different. Sometimes I even wonder if my dad still loves me. But he must, if he insisted on waiting until I get home to start trimming the tree.

"Get yourself some soup," Mom says.

"It smells so good," I say, dropping my backpack on a kitchen chair and getting a bowl from the cabinet.

"Now do we have to wait for Erica to *eat* before we start on the tree?" Rocky whines.

Mom laughs. "Bring your soup in the living room, Honey, so we can start on the tree. Rochelle's about to pop, she's in such a hurry."

The living room is filled with boxes of decorations, and presents, some wrapped and some not, and ribbon and wrapping paper strewn about. The tree is fresh and green and piney smelling.

"Here, Rocky," Dad says, holding out the white porcelain ornament of a tiny baby in a cradle that has Rocky's birthdate on it.

"You be first."

Rocky takes the ornament carefully from Dad and ties its red satin ribbon to a branch as high as she can reach. She stands back to admire it.

"Mine's prettier than yours," she says, sticking her tongue out at me.

"That's the old Christmas spirit," April laughs.

Dad hands my ornament to me. It's a crystal snowflake, and it has my name and birthdate engraved in the very center.

"Your grampa Arredondo sent this to you from Columbia on your very first Christmas," he tells me, as he has told me every year for as long as I can remember. "It was just before he died." He sighs. "I wish he could have lived long enough to see you girls."

The only grandparent I have is my gramma Schmidt—I never even saw any of the others, except in pictures. Every Christmas my dad tells us he wishes his parents could have lived long enough to see us. My mom wishes that for her father, too. I guess Christmas always reminds them of their earlier family times.

Dad digs around in the big box of Christmas decorations, unwrapping the tissue paper that keeps them clean and safe from year to year, searching.

"Gloria?" he says with a smile.

Mom reaches for the brass music scroll that says, "Gloria, in excelsis deo," which really means glory to God in the highest, but which Dad bought for Mom the first year they were married because it had her name on it.

Mom puts her ornament up high, just above Rocky's. Then Dad takes his Purple Heart out of the box and puts it next to Mom's. It's weird. He got that for being wounded in action, in Operation Desert Storm.

Whenever I ask him why he keeps it for the tree instead of wearing it on his dress uniform, he never gives me a straight answer. "They're called decorations, you know," he'll laugh, and then he changes the subject.

Dad searches around in the box some more, then comes up with a glass ornament in the shape of a raindrop. He hands it to April. She looks at him questioningly.

"April showers," he says.

We all laugh and she hangs the raindrop on the same branch as mine. Then we all start taking ornaments from the box and hanging them on the tree. We're finished in no time and we stand back to admire our work.

"It's beautiful," April says. "Our tree at home is all scraggly already."

"This is the prettiest tree we've ever had," Mom says. Which is also something she says every Christmas.

Dad turns off all the lights in the house, leaving only the Christmas tree lights on. We're all quiet, caught by the beauty of the moment. Dad puts his arm around me and pulls me close to him. I breathe deeply the mixed aromas of English Leather and pine tree, and I know my dad's not mad at me anymore. Rochelle puts her arm around Dad on the other side, and Mom comes to stand beside me, holding my hand.

"We should keep the tree up all year long," Rocky says.

The phone rings and I rush to answer it.

"Hey, Pups."

"Danny. Come over and see our tree. It's beautiful. Do you have a tree over there?"

"No. We were going to, but then nobody got around to it. Joey and I are putting lights up outside, though. It's a surprise for his mom."

"Come over when you're finished. We've got lots of albóndigas."

"Alex is keeping his car at home for awhile 'cause the cops won't leave him alone—so I don't have a way to get there."

"I can come get you. Okay?"

"So, okay. Come get me."

Danny's voice sounds a bit fuzzy.

"My parents will be mad at us all over again if they think you've been drinking before you come over."

Danny laughs. "Do you think I'm some kind of lightweight? They're not going to think I've been drinking."

"I don't want to think you've been drinking, either," I tell him.

"Hey, ease up. It's Christmas Eve. Besides, what makes you think I've been drinking? I'm cool."

"Okay. When will you be finished with the lights?"

"By the time you get here," Danny says.

"I'll be over in a few minutes then," I say, tapping the phone three times, I love you. Danny taps back, I love you, too, and we hang up.

April says she'll take me to get Danny, and, of course, Rocky wants to go too, and Kitty. Mom asks us to pick up some sweet potatoes at the market because she forgot them earlier. Then Dad asks us to go to Bixwell's drugstore for a special kind of candle he saw there the other day, and it would be nice to have "It's a Wonderful Life," to watch tomorrow night, so could we stop at the video store? Pretty soon we've got a whole list of errands.

When we get to Alex's I leave the others in the car and run in to get Danny. He and Joey are still working on getting the lights up around the windows at the front of the house. Joey is on a ladder and Danny is handing lights up to him. I kiss him on the lips. "Merry Christmas," I say, tasting alcohol on his breath.

"I'll be ready in a minute," Danny says. "We've just got two more windows to do. We want to finish before Gladys gets back."

I stand watching for awhile and see that two more windows will take longer than a minute. I walk back to the car.

"Danny's not ready yet. Why don't you and Rocky go on and get those things and then come back for us?"

"Okay," April says. "You think he'll be done in about twenty minutes?"

"I think so."

They drive off toward the drugstore, and I walk back to where Danny and Joey are working.

"Where's Alex?" I ask.

"He's at Gina's, trying to get back with her," Danny says.

"Stupid," Joey says, pounding a horseshoe nail into the window-sill, over the wire for the lights.

Danny laughs and hands the next section of wire and lights up to Joey. I notice Danny is weaving a bit.

"Hand up the Christmas cheer, too," Joey says.

Danny reaches for a bottle that's leaning against the side of the house. It's not one of those little Jack Daniels bottles. It's a big one, and there's not much left. Danny notices me looking at the bottle, but he just laughs.

Now I see that his eyes look dull, and he can hardly hold the bottle steady enough for Joey to reach down and take it. My heart sinks. Why does he do this? He can't go to my house like this. My parents would be totally freaked.

"How about if I make you some coffee?" I ask Danny.

"How about if I make you some coffee?" Joey mimics me in a shrill, mean voice.

"I'm not talking to you!" I yell at him.

"Yeah, coffee," Danny says.

I go into the kitchen, find the coffee can sitting on the sink, along with dirty dishes and food left over from breakfast, I guess—scrambled eggs, sticky in a skillet that will never be clean again. On the kitchen table there's a mustard jar and a catsup bottle that look as if they've been there for years, and utensils with dried food on them. I wash out the coffee pot, find a paper filter, and put in enough coffee to make an extra strong pot. I go back outside. Joey is off the ladder now, nailing lights along the sides of the window. Danny is sitting on the back steps, his head resting in his hands.

"Are you okay?" I ask.

Joey laughs. "Your boyfriend's a lightweight. You go for those lightweight types. Right?"

"Whatever," I say, keeping my attention on Danny.

"I'm fine," he mumbles. "Let's go to your house."

"And fags. You like the fags," Joey says.

"You need some coffee," I tell Danny. I know they say coffee doesn't really sober anyone up, but I'm hoping it will help anyway. I go back into the kitchen to check on it. Joey follows me inside. I ignore him and take a cup from the cabinet, then wash it out.

"You think our cups are too dirty for you?" Joey asks.

"Whatever," I say.

"Whatever. Whatever. Can't you even talk to me?"

"Why should I? You haven't said one nice thing to me since I've known you. You always act like you don't like me, so just leave me alone."

I start to pour coffee into the cup, but Joey grabs my arm.

"You like lightweights and faggots. I hate a girl who likes fuckin' faggots. I saw how you were, all laughing and happy with your faggot friend at the doggie jail."

"Let go of me!" I jerk my arm away, but he grabs it again. He pushes me backward, into the kitchen table.

"Leave me alone!" I scream.

He grabs my hair with his free hand, jerks my head backward, then shoves me against the table with the force of his body. His hand is wrapped tightly in my hair, pulling. I kick at him, trying to get free. He forces me onto my back, on the table. My head hits the jar of mustard. I squirm and push at him, trying to get up.

"What are you doing? Stop!"

I feel him heavy on top of me, grabbing at my jeans, pulling at the zipper. I twist, shove, kick, but I can't get away.

"You think you're somethin'. You ain't nothin'," he says, breathing stale whiskey into my face.

"Get away from me! Get off!" I buck hard, trying to move him, grab his hair to get his ugly face off of mine. Where's Danny?

"Danny!" I scream. "Danny!"

"Your lightweight can't help you now," Joey says, yanking my jeans down, tearing at my underwear.

I pull at his hair again. He grabs my arm. I lunge upward and bite his hand, hard.

"Bitch!"

He pulls his pants open in one quick move and I feel him ramming at me.

"Here's something you won't get from any faggot lightweight," he hisses at me.

I lunge and kick, trying to keep my legs closed tight. He jams his knee, hard, between my legs and then starts ramming again.

"Danny! Danny!" I scream at the top of my lungs, feeling a pain searing through my lower body, my head banging on the table. God! This isn't happening. "Danny!" I cry, kicking, losing strength.

Suddenly—a dog, Kitty, barking, April and Rocky, screaming. I see Kitty's muzzle, lunging at Joey's arm, clamping. April has her hands over Joey's face, pulling him backward while Rocky is pulling at his shirt. Kitty goes for Joey's neck. He grabs a knife from the table and swings at her. She falls back, then lunges again, this time sinking her teeth into his exposed butt. He screams and moves back. I roll over on my side, on the table, sobbing. That's when I see Danny standing in the doorway.

"What's going on?" he slurs.

Joey pulls the knife back, then jams it full force into Kitty's throat. She lets go. He raises the knife again, stabs again. Kitty, crouched down now, growls. Joey backs away.

April comes to me, helping me up.

"Get out of my house, you slut," Joey says to me.

April puts her arm around me. "Can you walk?" she whispers.

"I think so," I say, standing.

"Kitty," Rocky cries, bending down. "She's bleeding!"

"Get a towel," I tell her.

Rocky runs into the bathroom and comes out with a terrycloth towel. I lean down and tie the towel around Kitty's neck, firmly but not so tightly she can't breathe. I'm aware of a searing, stinging pain all through my vagina and lower abdomen, and a terrible pain at the back of my head, but somehow I move as if nothing's wrong, trying to help Kitty.

Joey has hobbled out of the room, gripping his butt. Danny comes to stand beside me.

"Are you okay, Pups?" he slurs.

Stupid question, I think, not answering. He just looks at me, confused.

I go back to one of the bedrooms and rip a sheet from the bed. We make a sort of hammock for Kitty and carry her to the car. Danny follows behind and stands watching as we pull away from Alex's house. I sit with Kitty in the back seat, applying pressure to her neck to try to slow the bleeding.

"The corner of Fourth and Jackson," I say, directing April to the emergency vet.

"You need a hospital, too," April says, driving like a maniac along Fourth Street.

"Not as much as Kitty does," I say.

The vet, Dr. Roberts, takes us in right away. I sit on the metal chair beside the examining table and Rocky and April stand next to Kitty.

Dr. Roberts calls an assistant in, and together they shave Kitty's neck.

"What happened here?"

"Someone stabbed her," April says.

"Why?"

"He was trying to get her to let go of him," I say.

"She was attacking him? If she was attacking him we've got to file a report and quarantine her."

"She was protecting my sister," Rocky says.

"Did she bite this guy? Did she break the skin?"

"No," April lies, flashing a look at Rocky.

Dr. Roberts looks over at me, as if he's noticed me for the first time.

"What happened to you? Are you okay?"

"I'm okay," I lie.

I sit hugging myself, trying to keep from shaking. I hurt all over.

Dr. Roberts gives Kitty a local anesthetic. "We've got a pretty extensive stitching job to do here, but she'll be all right," he says, looking over at me. "Why don't you go home? We're going to have to keep your dog for awhile, anyway."

"For Christmas?" Rocky says.

"Maybe longer if we have to quarantine her," the doctor says.

"Some Christmas," Rocky says, looking as if she might cry.

Christmas. I'd totally forgotten about Christmas. We get up to leave. April holds onto my arm and sort of guides me out the door.

"Are you sure you're okay?" the doctor asks.

"Sure," I say.

I sit in the front seat, suddenly cold. I can't stop shivering. April wants to take me to the hospital, but I only want to go home and soak in a hot bath. I've got to get clean. My head is spinning, with sharp pains jumping from back to front. I can't believe this happened to me. For the first time I think the word, rape.

My mom and dad are waiting for us when we get home, still in the holiday spirit.

"What took you so long?" Mom asks, smiling. "Where's Danny?"

I watch her smile fade as she gets a closer look at me. I don't know what I look like but I can tell it's not good just by watching the expressions on my parents' faces.

"What's happened?" Dad says.

Everyone starts talking at once—everyone but me, that is. I sink onto the couch, numb. Dad sits beside me and puts his arms around me and holds me tight. I start crying, shaking with sobs, shivering with cold. Dad gets a blanket from the linen closet and wraps it around me. "Oh Holy Night" is playing on the stereo. Mom is sitting next to me, looking at my face, the back of my head, asking where I'm hurt.

"I want to take a bath," I choke out through trembling lips.

"Not yet," Dad says.

My mom goes into the next room and picks up the phone. I hear her say, "My daughter's been raped."

Rape, I think. Rape. Then we are all getting into the car and going to the hospital. It is just after midnight. Christmas morning.

=16=

$\mathbf{A}$n attendant is waiting for us at the hospital emergency entrance.

"Erica Arredondo?"

I nod.

"Are you her mother?" she asks, turning to Mom.

"Yes."

"Come back with her, if you'd like. The rest of you can wait here, or in the main waiting room upstairs," she says.

"I'll go, too," Dad says.

"Only one. You or the mom."

"I'll go, Grant," Mom says.

The attendant, Cindy Nguyen according to her name tag, hands Dad a clipboard with a bunch of forms on it.

"I'll need you to fill out these papers. When the police get here they'll want to interview all of you, so stick around."

"Don't worry," Dad says. "I definitely want to talk to the police."

The attendant leads me and Mom down the hall and into an examining room. The equipment in here is not unlike that in the Humane Society surgery room, an EKG, a breathing monitor, a high, narrow table. But the table in here has a mattress pad on it, instead of being bare metal. And stirrups. This table has stirrups.

The attendant motions for us to sit down and pulls a chair up opposite us.

"My name is Cindy," she says, extending her hand first to Mom and then to me.

"We try to make this as easy as possible, but nothing is easy at a time like this, is it?" she says with a smile.

I've still got the blanket from home wrapped around me, and I'm still shivering.

"Let me explain the general procedure to you . . . In a potentially criminal case, it's important that evidence be gathered in the proper manner, so a police officer with special training will be here soon to monitor procedures. Also, because rape victims often feel further victimized by the system, someone from the Rape Crisis Center will be here . . ."

Cindy talks on and on, while I feel myself removed, watching as if from a distance, as if this is all happening to someone else.

"Erica. Erica," Mom says, touching me gently on the shoulder.

"Cindy's talking to you."

Cindy is holding a hospital gown in front of me.

"Step into that little room and take your clothes off. Put this on with the opening in the back."

"I have to go to the bathroom first," I say.

"Sorry, that has to wait until after the examination. It shouldn't be long now."

I go into the room and start to take off my clothes. My mom stands at the doorway, watching, teary. My shirt is stained with blood. Kitty's, I think. My jeans are torn at the waist. My underpants are sticky with a combination of my blood and Joey's cum, a repulsive, dark gummy fluid, of the sort Gregor Samsa dirtied his room with. The sight, the acrid odor, sickens me. I retch up the soup from a happier time. Mom is suddenly beside me, holding me, wiping my mouth with the blouse I've just removed.

Cindy comes to the door with paper towels and a damp washcloth.

"Oh, no," she says, seeing the blouse in Mom's hand and taking it from her. "This is evidence," she says, gathering it and the rest of my clothes up and placing them in a plastic bag.

"Here—just your face," she says, handing me the washcloth.

I wipe my mouth, wanting desperately to wipe between my legs, to wipe Joey away, but Cindy is watching me as if she knows my mind.

Mom holds the hospital gown up for me and I slip my arms into it. She leads me to the examining table and I lie down. She tucks the blanket from home around me and Cindy brings a hospital blanket to put over that. I am still shivering. I think I may never feel warm again. I've forgotten what it's like to feel warm.

It is all a blur to me, the policewoman, the woman from the Rape Crisis Center, questions, murmurs of reassurance.

The doctor, also a woman, gives me an injection that she says will not put me out, but help me relax. Something like the pre-anesthetic we give the animals before spaying, I think. Maybe I'm going to be spayed, my ovaries and womb turned into fertilizer, I imagine, under the slight haze of a relaxing drug.

The doctor first apologizes, then pokes and prods where I've already been poked and prodded, where I hurt. Mom holds my hand and the policewoman writes information on a clipboard while blood samples and fluid samples and scrapings are collected from me. The doctor combs my pubic hair with a fine-tooth comb, to gather possible pubic hair from the rapist, she tells me. I think it's me. I'm not sure. I'm keeping my distance.

"You can use the bathroom now," the doctor says, calling me from my hazy world.

Mom walks with me down the hall. "Do you want me to come in with you?"

I shake my head no.

"Well, I'll be right out here if you need me."

I use the toilet, then soak paper towels in hot water, douse them with liquid soap, and scrub between my legs. It is not enough. I need a shower. A bath. A cleansing that is beyond anything I know of.

Back in the examining room, Jenny, from the Rape Crisis Center, hands me a clean pair of underpants and a set of sweats.

"Loaners," she says. "Wash them and bring them back to the center some time. No hurry."

"Thank you," Mom says for me.

I get dressed and we walk out to the waiting room to get the others. Jenny follows behind us.

The policewoman is there, asking April and Rocky some questions. I now notice it's Officer Wright, the one who lectured me when I got taken in with Danny and Alex that time.

I sit down next to my dad, who puts his arm around me and pulls me close.

"Okay?" he whispers.

I nod, though I have no idea what okay might feel like after all this.

"Let's finish this another time," Dad says, standing. "I want to get Erica home. She's been through enough."

"April, when I write this report I'd like you to come look it over, be sure we've got everything down that you witnessed."

"Sure," April says.

We all stand to leave. Officer Wright gives me a long look.

"Didn't I tell you?"

I just look at her.

"Lie down with dogs, get up with fleas," she says.

Jenny jumps between me and Wright. "That was totally uncalled for, Officer!"

Wright just shrugs her shoulders and walks away.

At home Mom runs a hot bath for me and sits on the closed toilet while I bathe.

"I'm okay, Mom. You can leave."

"The doctor said you'd be groggy from the shot for awhile. I don't think it's safe for you to be in the bathtub unattended."

I want to wash in private places. I don't want a witness, not even my mom. I guess she figures it out because she stands up and says, "I'm going to go kiss Rochelle goodnight, then I'll come back and check on you."

In the middle of the night I hear the phone ring and my father's voice. Is it a dream? I'm so buried under layers of fog I'm not sure. At first it is only mumbling, then Dad's voice rising.

"NO! I won't wake her to come to the phone!"

There is a slam of the receiver, and all is quiet again. I reach my feet to the end of the bed, reaching for the warmth of the sleeping Kitty, only to find the eerie lightness of a blanket over my feet. Kitty? Memory returns for an instant and then I will myself to sink again.

"**M**erry Christmas doesn't quite fit the occasion, does it?" my dad asks, sitting on the edge of my bed and gently rubbing my back.

I open my eyes to a sun-filled room. The blinds on my windows are open, showing it to be a California-Christmas kind of day, brisk, but bright. Already I hear the kids from next door riding new bikes around the cul-de-sac.

"Eleven," Dad says. "We thought it was time to rouse you."

I get up and take a long, hot shower and wash my hair again, even though I did that not more than seven hours ago. I check myself in the mirror. Not much shows. A big bruise on my arm, a small bruise on my cheek, a cut on my hand, a nail broken past the quick. Nothing to indicate the change in me. I had expected to see a reflection of a huge beetle when I stood before the mirror, but no.

In the living room, Dad and Mom and Rocky sit waiting for me, Rocky not even complaining about holding off on the opening of gifts for so long.

"I miss Kitty," she says, looking at the traditional package on the tree that contains a new ball with a bell in it.

That's the Christmas routine. Kitty runs around, bouncing her ball, happily ringing the bell all the while we open gifts.

Suddenly I remember what Dr. Roberts said about possibly quarantining Kitty.

"I'll be right back," I say.

I go into my room and rummage through my backpack and find my little book with telephone numbers in it, then dial Dr. Franz's home phone.

She answers, "Merry Christmas."

"I need your help."

"Erica?"

I tell her an abridged version of what happened last night, going light on the gory details.

"What a terrible experience for you."

In the background I hear the strains of "Jingle Bells," and laughter. I get to the point.

"Kitty shouldn't have to be quarantined for protecting me."

"That's standard procedure," Dr. Franz says.

"I know, but, could you help me get her out?"

There is a long silence on the phone, then she asks the name of the vet who treated Kitty last night.

"Dr. Roberts."

"Gray hair? A little thin mustache?"

"Yeah."

"Well . . . I know her rabies vaccination is up to date because I personally inoculated her at last month's clinic . . . Still, anytime a dog bites someone . . ."

"Please," I say.

Another long pause, then, "I'll see what I can do."

"I know you're busy with Christmas and all . . ."

"Don't worry about that. Are you going to be okay?"

"It will help if we can get Kitty back."

"I'll try."

We open presents with Christmas music playing on the stereo. Gramma and some of my parents' friends come for dinner. People talk and laugh and eat. Rocky sings "Oh Holy Night" for everyone, sometime between dinner and dessert. It looks like Christmas and it sounds like Christmas, but it doesn't feel like Christmas to me.

I read a book once about people who'd had near-death experiences, and how, when their hearts had stopped and they were totally unconscious, they floated serenely above the scene, seeing their own motionless bodies below, and watching the activity all around them. That's how it is for me right now. I'm floating, disconnected.

Several times during the day the phone rings. Dad always answers it. Sometimes it's a friend from far away, and I hear him say "Merry Christmas to you, too." A few times he answers but no one is on the other end. Just after we finish dinner, April calls.

"Do you want to come to the phone?" Dad asks.

"I'll call her tomorrow," I say, feeling too drained of energy even to talk to April.

"She'll be okay," I hear my dad say. "She's been through a lot. But April, thank you. Things would have been much, much worse if you hadn't shown up when you did."

All during the day, my parents reach out to touch me as I walk by, or one of them sits next to me when I sit down. "Are you okay?" they ask, time and again. Always I nod yes.

Rocky doesn't pester me to play any of her new games with her. Sometimes I catch her looking at me, not full on, but out of the corner of her eye—like Gregor Samsa's sister must have looked at him when he first became a beetle.

Just before dark Dr. Franz arrives with Kitty, who walks in and sits at my feet.

"Will you have some dessert with us?" Mom asks.

"Thanks, I can't stay. I'll just say hello to Erica."

Dr. Franz comes in and pulls a chair up beside me.

"I'm sorry this happened to you," she says.

I nod my head. What is there to say?

Rocky gets Kitty's package from the tree, opens the package and rolls the ball to her. Kitty looks at it without interest.

"She's sedated," Dr. Franz says. "I promised Dr. Roberts you'd keep her home for two weeks. Don't even take her for a walk on a leash."

══ **17** ══

I soak in the bathtub, shower after, and still I'm not clean. It's as if I've been permanently stained by Joey. Brushing my hair, I feel the tenderness of my scalp, where he grabbed my hair and yanked my head backward.

When I crawl into bed, Kitty climbs up and lies at my feet. I check out the stitches on her shaved neck—thirty-seven in all. I reach down to pet her and she inches her way up beside me.

"Thank you," I tell her, remembering how she didn't let up on Joey, even after he hurt her.

Shifting and turning in bed, I try to get comfortable, my bruises and the tears within me more intense than they were earlier. Why did this happen to me? I try to remember everything I've ever heard about rape, that it's an act of violence, not sexual, that it's never the victim's fault, that women who've been raped are often treated as if *they're* the guilty parties if a case goes to court. I also remember hearing that most rapes are perpetrated by someone who is known to the victim.

Victim. Is that what I am? Someone who falls into the faceless victim category?

What could I have done? Gone for the eyes? But I couldn't get loose. Been stronger? It was a little late to start pumping iron right then. Not washed a coffee cup? Not been seen talking with Sinclair? Not have a drunk for a boyfriend?

I turn on my side, my knees bent, my back resting against the weight of Kitty. Images of Joey keep intruding, his angry face over mine, the stench of stale whiskey, his grip on my hair, the tight clutching of his fingers around my wrist, his weight on top of me. I try to think of other things, to remove myself, and finally it works. My sad soul rises, detaches, and settles a safe distance above my bruised body.

Long after traffic noises have died down and our house is totally quiet, I hear a pounding on the front door. Kitty jumps from the bed, barking, her bristles raised. I get up and open my bedroom door and let Kitty run down the hall to the front door, then I go back to bed and curl up like a ball.

I hear my dad stirring around.

The pounding is steady and loud.

"Who's there?" Dad yells, over Kitty's barking.

"Gladys Kendall! I need to talk to you!"

"Gladys Kendall?—Shut up, Kitty—Erica, call Kitty."

I call Kitty and get her back to my room.

"Joey Kendall's mother!" I hear, and then more pounding.

"Don't open the door, Grant," Mom says, but Dad unbolts the lock. Gladys comes in.

"They've arrested my son. On Christmas Day they came and arrested my son."

I can tell from the fuzzy, running-together words that Gladys is in her usual half-drunk, or more, state.

"You've got to drop the charges," she pleads.

"Not in *my* lifetime!" Dad says.

Me. The words are about me, but I don't let them in. I listen, but only on the outside.

"It's all a big mistake," Gladys Kendall says through muffled sobs. "Where's Erica? I want to talk to Erica."

"Erica's been through enough," Mom says.

"Please, give Joey a chance . . . He's not a bad boy," Gladys says, sounding like a drunken version of some mother from an old melodramatic movie.

I hear my mom's voice, and then Gladys Kendall's, but their

words aren't clear to me.

Then, louder, "What good does it do to arrest him? What's done is done . . . please. He didn't mean anything by it."

"He meant plenty!" Dad says.

"It's so hard on him to be locked up again."

"Hard on *him*?" my dad yells. "Do you think I give a shit about *him*? We've just spent hours at the hospital with Erica and it's only the beginning . . ."

And now, everyone is talking at once, no one really listening.

"Grant, don't bother, this woman won't even remember . . ."

"My sons are all I've got . . ."

"She could be pregnant, or diseased, or God knows . . ."

"Calm down, Grant, this won't help . . ."

"And the emotional scars . . ."

" . . . not such a big deal. Sex is just an everyday thing to your daughter, in case you didn't know . . . "

"Get out!" Mom yells.

I hear scuffling, and then the door slams, hard, shaking the house like an earthquake. I pull the covers back over my head.

Mom comes in to check on me early in the afternoon.

"I thought I heard you up and around," she says.

"I got up for a bath, but then I got back in bed."

She checks the bruise on my arm and the one on my cheek.

"How are you feeling, Sweetheart?"

"Okay. I'm just so . . . tired, or something."

"Do you hurt anywhere?"

"Not really," I say, though that's not exactly the truth. It's more like I hurt in my deepest self, but I don't know how to tell her that.

"Dad and I told Gramma we'd pick up a few groceries for her. Why don't you get up and come with us? It might do you good to get out."

I shake my head no. "I really don't feel like it, Mom."

"Well, I hate to leave you alone. Rocky's over at Jessica's."

"I'll be fine," I tell her.

"Do you want me to stay? Dad can take care of the groceries."

"No, really, go ahead."

"Someone's been calling again today and hanging up when we answer," Mom says. "Dad thinks it's Danny and that he's afraid to talk to either of us. Don't answer the phone if you don't want to."

I nod.

She sits looking at me, worried.

"Can I get you anything before we leave?"

"No. Thanks."

"Well . . . we won't be gone long. You've got your partner," she says, reaching to pet Kitty. "What a good dog you've been . . . She's hardly left your side all day, has she?"

"Just once, to go outside."

No sooner have my parents backed out the driveway than the phone rings.

"Pups?"

"Danny. Oh, Danny," I say, crying, wanting his arms around me.

"I've been trying to reach you for the last two days. I had a Christmas present for you and everything . . . I tried to call . . ."

"You did?"

"Well, but your dad kept answering the phone. I wanted *you* to answer . . . Listen, Pups. What happened? All I know is Kitty got Joey good, and then you were leaving without saying good-bye or anything . . ."

"You really don't know?"

"I just know *something* happened. I know Joey was arrested and that he's charged with assault and rape and Gladys is going nuts."

I am beyond tears now, shocked. He doesn't know what happened? The memory of Danny, drunk, standing in the doorway after Joey'd rammed inside me in that most personal, violent way, flashes before me—Danny, asking what was going on.

"I guess I was a little out of it," he says.

"God, Danny. I was raped. Joey raped me. While you were just outside the door. While I was screaming to you for help! I was RAPED!"

There is a long silence, then, "I'm sorry, Pups. I'm sorry. Are you okay now? I mean, he didn't beat you up or anything, did he?"

"Fine. I'm *fine* now. I was *only* raped. Not beaten—at least not too bad," I say, all sarcastic.

Another long silence. Then Danny says, "I told you he was crazy, didn't I?"

"You didn't tell me he might just up and decide to rape me!"

"Erica, I feel bad, I really do. But what can I do now?"

"Nothing. There's nothing you can do," I say, feeling defeated, wanting only to go back to the safety of my room, to curl up in a ball and pull the covers tight around me.

"How about if I bring your present over late tonight, after your parents are in bed . . . We don't have to do anything, you know, sexy or anything, if you don't want to."

"How sensitive of you," I say, sarcastic again. "I've lost the Christmas spirit."

"Tomorrow night?"

"I don't think so."

"When?"

"I don't know."

"I'll call you tomorrow then. Answer the phone, will you?"

"I don't know," I say, and hang up.

For the rest of Christmas vacation I spend a lot of time in my room. It's where I feel safe. I listen to music and read a James Herriot book, *All Creatures Great and Small*. James Herriot was a vet in England who worked with pigs and cows and sheep, in addition to the usual dog and cat clientele. I've read all of his books at least once. They're safe, too.

I ask my mom to call the Humane Society and tell them I'm sick. I've never done that before, but I just don't want to leave the house.

Mom and Dad keep trying to get me to go out with them, to a movie, or for pizza, things we've always done together, but I have no heart for it. I know they're concerned, and trying to be nice, but mostly I want to be left alone, in my room.

The Sunday before school starts April drops by. We sit out on my front steps, talking. Kitty sits next to me, leaning her chin on my leg.

"Here, I got this for you," April says, handing me something that looks like a little hairspray can.

"Pepper spray," she explains. "After what happened to you, I decided never to be without it, and you shouldn't either," she says, dangling a can from her key chain.

"Where'd you get it?"

"My dad got it for me—one squirt and guys like Joey'll be stopped cold."

"Thanks," I say.

"Any news about the hearing?"

I shake my head. "They haven't set a date yet."

"You know who called me last night?" April says.

It's one of those questions that requires no answer.

"Danny Lara."

"Oh?" I say.

"He was *all* upset—says he can't get through to you, you don't answer the phone—he asked me to talk to you."

I pick up a rock and toss it a few feet away. Kitty bounds over and picks it up, then brings it back to me.

"Are you breaking up with him, or what?"

"I don't know. It's like I can't think straight right now. When the phone rings, I don't answer it. I'm not even sure why. I just don't feel like talking."

"He was on this kick about how he was no good, he felt so guilty. I felt kind of sorry for him. We talked for a long time."

"Did he ask how I was doing?"

April looks at me, thoughtful. "No, not really. Mostly he talked about how awful he felt."

"Do you think he'd been drinking?"

"Maybe. He sounded all emotional when he was telling me how guilty he felt, couldn't sleep, couldn't eat. Once I even thought he might be crying."

"He does that sometimes, if he's had a lot to drink. Or . . ." I think about how he always cried after sex, like those were the only times he could express any emotions—with drinking or sex.

"Or what?" April asks.

"I forgot what I was going to say," I tell her.

"Anyway, he wants you to call him . . . Do you think you will?"

"I don't know," I say, which seems to be my answer to almost everything these days.

Monday morning I get up and get ready for school, but at the last minute I decide not to go. My bruises are gone, and I'm not so sore inside anymore, but . . . I just don't feel like going. Rocky does though, and when she gets home she comes into my room. I'm stretched out on my bed reading *All Things Bright and Beautiful.* Rocky closes the door behind her and then searches through her backpack.

"Here, this is for you," she whispers, taking out a brown envelope and handing it to me.

"Why are you whispering?"

"It's from Danny."

"How'd you get it?"

"He waited for me after school and handed it to me. He said to tell you he really misses you."

Rocky stands watching me. "Aren't you going to open it?"

"Not until you leave," I tell her.

"Why not?"

"Maybe it's a bomb," I say, sarcastically.

"No way. You just don't want me to see it."

"So? Leave."

"I'll tell Mom you've got a package from Danny," Rocky says.

"Tell her. I don't care."

Rocky leaves, reluctantly, and goes out to the kitchen. I hear the refrigerator door and know Rocky has other things on her mind now.

I open the package and take out my silver barrette and a letter from Danny. It says,

Dear Pups,

Here's your barrette. I found it under the table. I've got to talk to you. Why won't you come to the phone? I guess you think I let you down. I feel so awful about what happened, but that's over now. I just want things back the way they were.

I really need to talk to you. Please, Erica, I feel so lonely without you. Can I come to your window tonight? I'll be way quiet, so the Green Beret man won't hear a thing. I'm going nuts. I need to feel you next to me.

I love you,

Danny

I read the letter twice. I'm suddenly so angry that every little bit of the floating feeling leaves me and I'm grounded in the reality I've been trying to avoid. I grab a pen and notebook paper and start writing.

Dear Danny,

I can't believe you! I've just been through the most horrible experience of my life. And you didn't even help me. You were too drunk! And now, in your letter, there's not one word of concern for me. You feel, you want, you need, YOU, YOU, YOU, BUT WHAT ABOUT ME? WHAT ABOUT ME, DANNY?

I'm hurt bad, and I don't exactly know where to go from here but one thing I do know, what you feel or want or need is not coming first with me anymore. Another thing. Here's your ring back. It feels like a lie to me. And don't come knocking at my window.

Erica

I almost sign "love, Erica" out of habit, but love's not what I'm feeling. I take my ring off and wrap the letter around it. I put them in an envelope and seal it.

I take the scissors from my desk drawer and look in the mirror for a long time. Hardly an hour passes that I don't feel Joey clutching my hair, pulling my head back, grabbing at me, ramming at me, overpowering me. I take the scissors and cut a hunk of hair close to my scalp. I watch the shiny black hair fall to the floor, then grab another clump. Never again. Never again, I think as I cut another handful, and another as fast as I can, with no regard for evenness, my only thought that no one now will be able to grab a handful of my hair and use that maneuver against me.

When I'm done, I pick up the silver barrette, turn away from the mirror, and step through mounds of hair to get to my dresser. There I remove the T-shirt which wraps the can of foam and my one remaining condom. I add the barrette to the other two items and wrap the shirt back up. I place the bundle beneath my other shirts, in the far back corner of my bottom drawer, where it will remain unopened, a remnant from an earlier life, like the picture books stored on my closet shelf.

"**E**rica?"

Dad stands looking at me, shocked. He reaches to the floor and picks up a handful of my hair, and when he stands again I see tears in his eyes.

"Why?" he asks, fingering the hair.

"Oh, Daddy."

"E.J., E.J." he says, holding me tightly while I cry against his chest, comforted by the rough fabric of his wool shirt, and the aroma of English Leather.

"It's okay, it's okay," he says, over and over, until I'm not certain if he's talking to me, or to himself.

18

Walking into the Humane Society, I feel all eyes on me. I go from the reception desk, past the infirmary, out to the kennels and Beauty—always my first stop of the day. She stands on her hind legs, sticking her white-trimmed nose through the chain-link fence, wagging her tail frantically.

"Hi, Beauty. Hi, girl," I say, opening the gate to her kennel and walking inside. She runs in close circles around my legs. I kneel down and pet her, laughing.

"You've missed me, huh? Has anyone exercised you this week?"

She licks my face, not seeming to notice my lack of hair. I attach her leash and walk her out into the alleyway, where we go for a brisk walk. I used to have to urge her on, she would tire so easily. Now it's as if Beauty has the stamina to walk forever. She sets the pace and I lag.

We walk past a trash barrel that has a crusty old jar of mustard sitting on top of other trash. Joey's house, the table, the helplessness, Joey's intrusion into my body, all brought back to me, in a flash, by a discarded mustard jar. I stop, leaning against a cement block wall. Beauty looks at me, confused by my sudden halt, then strains at the leash.

"In a minute," I say, and she stands on her hind legs, her front paws on my upper thighs. She looks at me, wagging her tail, then gets back on all fours, again pulling at the leash.

"Okay, okay," I say, starting off in a jog back to the Humane Society.

Sinclair walks past Beauty's kennel as I'm putting her back. He stops.

"My God, girl. I didn't even recognize you at first," he says. "Love your hair . . . " He starts in a joking manner but his smile fades quickly. "Are you okay?" he asks.

I nod my head yes.

"When your mom called to say you wouldn't be in last week she said you weren't feeling well."

"The flu," I explain.

I see that Sinclair is looking me over carefully, the way he might a new animal who isn't quite right, but no one knows exactly what's wrong.

"Beauty's looking good," I say, anxious to direct attention away from me.

"I wouldn't have given a nickel for her life when Antoinette first brought her in—you've done a great job with her."

We both stand looking at the healthy dog who only a month ago couldn't even hold her head up. Couldn't or wouldn't. Now she stands strong and alert, ears perked, tail wagging tentatively, hoping for another walk.

"I've got to get back to work. The volunteers' schedule is a mess—glad you're back."

"Me, too," I say, then walk back to the infirmary to see what's needed for the health team today.

Dr. Franz does a double take when she sees me. "New groomer?" she laughs.

"Yeah," I say, smiling.

She turns me around, checks out the back of my hair, then says, "It makes sense to me . . . let's get to work."

The time goes quickly—three cats spayed, four dogs inoculated, information recorded on charts, cages disinfected—it's good to be busy.

At the end of the day when I go to Sinclair's office to sign out he tells me he's been waiting for me. He holds a set of electric clippers, the kind we use to clip the dogs with.

"Sterilized and everything," he says. "Here, sit here." He motions to the high desk chair that sits in front of the computer.

At first I have no idea what he's getting at, but when he drapes a towel around my neck it becomes obvious that he has plans for my hair.

"Let me just even this up a bit. I'm good with the scissors and shears."

He takes the mirror out of the parrot's cage and hands it to me. "You can watch," he says.

"I don't think so," I tell him.

"Have I ever steered you wrong?" he says, pretending to be hurt.

I look at the raggedy lengths of my hair, and suddenly, real as anything, I see Joey's image in the mirror, my hair long again, his hand wrapped in it, pulling.

"Well, have I?" Sinclair says.

"What?"

"C'mon, girl, stay with me here. Have I ever steered you wrong?"

"No."

"Well, then, let me straighten the peaks and valleys of what was once your shining glory."

What can it hurt? I don't care, anyway.

"Okay," I tell him, setting the mirror down on the table.

Sinclair runs his hands through my hair. "What happened to you?"

"I was tired of long hair."

"So you just hacked away at it?"

"Exactly."

Sinclair looks at me for a minute, puzzled, then he turns on the clippers. I close my eyes, hearing the buzz, like a swarm of mosquitoes around my ears.

"Better, huh?" Sinclair says, holding the mirror up in front of me.

"I guess."

"No. Look! It *is*!"

He gets some hair gel from his bottom drawer and rubs some through my hair, making it stand on end. It's no longer than Dr. Franz's now.

"A fashion statement! I like it!"

I smile, not caring about a fashion statement but knowing

Sinclair is trying to help.

"Color would help," he says. "Either total blond, or something bright, maybe a pink or chartreuse."

"Right," I say, taking off the towel and getting my backpack from my locker.

"Think about color!" Sinclair calls after me as I walk out the door and to the front parking lot where my mom is waiting.

After dinner we're all still sitting around the table when the phone rings.

"Erica, it's Jenny, from the Rape Crisis Center," Mom says.

I shake my head no, but Mom just keeps holding the phone out to me, so finally I take it.

"How're you doing?" Jenny asks.

"Okay," I say.

"How about if I come get you—take you out for a bite to eat or something?"

"I just ate," I tell her.

"Well . . . I'd like to talk with you. When would be a good time?"

I pause, not wanting to commit myself but not knowing how to get out of it.

"Maybe tomorrow?"

"How about later this evening? Maybe around eight? It won't take long."

"Okay," I say, not knowing how to get out of it.

Mom looks at me questioningly.

"She wants to talk to me," I say.

Mom follows me back to my room.

"I'm glad Jenny called," Mom says. I sit down in my desk chair and Mom stands behind me, rubbing my back like she used to do when I was little.

"I think it's probably a good idea for you to talk with her . . ." She stops rubbing my back. "What happened to the picture of you and Danny you always had here on your desk?"

"I put it away."

"Erica, I'm sorry, Honey, I know we've been through this all before and you don't really want to talk more about it, but . . . Danny

. . . he wasn't involved in any way, was he, in the, you know, what Joey did to you?"

"No."   ‚

"Well, what . . ."

"I can't be with Danny anymore," I say. And then, before I can get away from myself, lift out of my body and watch, a wave of sadness comes over me, body and soul, and tears pour down my cheeks.

Mom steps in front of me and pulls my head against her chest, petting my short, short hair.

"I'm so sorry this happened to you," she whispers. "So, so, sorry."

"He didn't help me, Mom. I thought we loved each other. I thought we would always be there for each other, and he was so drunk he didn't even know what was happening."

Mom reaches over to my bedside table and hands me a bunch of tissue.

"I've thought about it a lot—it was just a pretend love."

"What do you mean?"

"If someone loves you, they help you when you need help, right?"

"Right," Mom says, rubbing my back again.

"Well, Danny was just like—he didn't have a clue. I tried so hard to help him with his mom's death and all, and then, when I needed him most of all, he wasn't there . . ."

I gasp, trying to catch my breath, wanting to stop crying but not knowing how.

Jenny arrives at exactly 8:00. She's driving an old Volkswagen—beetle style. She takes me to the Tasty Grinder and orders an espresso. I just get a glass of water. We sit at a back table.

"I want to encourage you to start meeting with the group I lead at the YWCA," Jenny tells me.

"Why?"

"You've been through a very traumatic experience. It helps to talk about things with other women who've been in similar situations."

"You mean everyone in the group has been raped?"

"Well, or abused one way or another."

"I don't *want* to talk about it. I just want to forget it."

"And how's that going? Are you forgetting?"

"Most of the time," I say.

"Those other times are the pits though, aren't they?"

"Sort of."

"Look, Erica. You'll get past this more quickly if you work through some things in a group. Just give it a try. If you don't like it, you can always quit."

Jenny hands me a card with the times and places for group meetings.

I thank her for the card, even though I don't plan on attending any meetings. Why keep talking about something that's been done, that can never be undone? There'll be plenty of time for that at the trial. If it comes to a trial.

After I stay home from school for a week, my mom and dad have one of those long, insistent talks with me. What it boils down to is I either start getting myself to school or they'll drag me.

April picks me up in the car her dad got her for Christmas. Any other time I'd be at least a little jealous—like I used to be over April's very own state-of-the-art home entertainment system, and her very own telephone and answering machine. But now—nothing much touches me right now.

Everybody makes a big deal about my hair. That's okay. Maybe it keeps them from seeing inside me. Maybe they won't see the girl who's been raped if they mainly notice my hair.

"Welcome back," Ms. Lee tells me as I take my seat in English. "Did you get your hair cut?" she asks.

The whole class laughs but I think it's a sincere question coming from her. She's so involved in literature she barely notices real life. Maybe she's got the right idea. Real life doesn't seem so great to me right now.

"Come see me after class and I'll tell you about make-up assignments."

By the end of fourth period, I've got three pages of make-up assignments to do.

Walking back from gym to Peer Counseling, someone down the hall yells "FAGGOT!" First, I freeze. Then the tears start. Without a plan, without a thought, I step into a narrow space between two temporary buildings. The tardy bell has rung, the halls are quiet, and I'm still standing there, sobbing, trying to catch my breath, while "FAGGOT" echoes in my head.

"What's up?"

I jump at the voice of the campus supervisor.

"You're a mess," he tells me, and then makes a call on his Walkie-Talkie thing. "Joyce, can you meet me near the fence, between B-1 and B-2?"

When Joyce arrives, the other guy leaves saying, "I bet this is a girl thing."

Joyce walks me to the restroom and hands me some damp paper towels for my face.

"What's wrong?" she asks.

"Nothing," I tell her.

"Just out there watering the lawn with your tears, were you?"

"That's it," I say, all sarcastic.

"Come on, I'll walk with you to the counselor's office."

"I'm okay now. I'll just go to class."

"Nope. You have to check in with a counselor first."

Ms. Security walks me to the office, talks with Ms. Wong for a minute, then motions me inside.

"I'm glad you're here," Ms. Wong says. "I've been planning to call you in anyway."

I suppose she means my slipping grades, or my recent absence, I don't know.

"Tell me about your hair," she says, looking me over carefully.

"There's nothing to tell. I just decided it was too long . . . Can I go back to class now?"

She smiles. "Then tell me what brought you to tears this afternoon."

It's not that I don't like Ms. Wong. It's just that, right now, I'd rather keep my problems to myself. I wish there were somewhere I could go, a cave or something, where no one would know where I was, and no one would be asking, "What happened to your hair?"

or "Are you okay?" or any of that well-meaning stuff that I don't know how to answer.

"Erica? You were crying?"

"I can't exactly explain it," I say. And that's the truth.

19

"**E**rica?"

Danny steps out from the shadows of the building as I'm walking to the pet adoption van.

I stop, stunned by the familiarity of his voice.

He looks at me, frowning. "Your hair . . . " He pauses, seeming not to know how to finish the sentence. Then he says, "I've got to talk to you."

"I've only got a minute before the van leaves."

"Then give me a minute."

"Okay," I say. I sit down on a bench and look up at him, waiting.

He is wearing a white T-shirt and jeans, with a new pair of boots, and he looks as if he's fresh from the shower.

"I love you, Erica. I don't know what else to say."

"I can't be with you anymore," I tell him.

"But Erica, Pups, all I'm asking is a chance," he pleads. "You'll see. I'll even stop drinking if you want me to, if that's it."

"It's too late, Danny. Too much has happened."

He sits down next to me and tries to pull me to him. A part of me wants to melt into him, but I sit straight, maintaining a distance.

"It can't be too late," he whispers.

"It is."

"Just give it a try," he says, tears welling in his eyes.

"I'm all dead inside," I tell him. "I couldn't try if I wanted to."

"But . . . "

"I always was there for you, whenever you needed me. And then . . . It's no use . . . I've got to go now," I tell him, getting up from the bench and walking away.

He follows me to the van. I can feel him watching me as I open the door, then I hear his footsteps crunching down the alley as he walks away. I sit on the upholstered bench opposite the driver's seat and desperately fight to keep from crying about all that can never be. I try to do my trick of leaving my body and just hovering overhead but I can't get away from me. All I know to do is hold my breath, tight, to freeze my tears inside.

Sinclair gets in the van, carrying the last animal with him. It is a Siamese cat with a meow like fingernails on a chalkboard. He puts her in a cage, buckles up and starts the engine.

"I really appreciate your making time to help with another mobile pet adoption," Sinclair says. "I don't know how in the world we'll get along without you next year when you're off to college."

His words, the warmth of his smile, melt my hardened tears free. I turn away, trying to hide my face from him, but Sinclair is not easy to fool. He shuts off the engine and moves over beside me, sitting with his shoulder touching mine.

"What did I say?"

I shake my head no as I wipe tears away.

"This is about more than missing us when you go away," he says.

Yes, I nod.

"Danny?"

I shrug my shoulders.

"Look, Erica, I see that things are different for you since you've come back from having the flu, or whatever. I don't want to be nosy, and you don't have to tell me a thing. But sometimes it helps to talk about things."

I nod.

"Remember that night we sat in your driveway, and I told you how I wasn't welcome with my family at their holiday parties?"

"I remember."

"That meant a lot to me—that you listened to me and didn't judge me."

I wipe my face again and try to control my breathing.

"I can listen," Sinclair says.

I nod.

We sit like that, shoulder to shoulder, hearing the animals shuffle around in their cages, and the grating sound of the cat, until Sinclair looks at his watch.

"We'll be late," he says, and gets back in the driver's seat.

When we return and unload the animals, I stop to say good-night to Beauty.

"We should take her on the next trip," Sinclair says. "She's healthy now, and looking good—just about eligible for adoption."

"Beauty?"

"Yeah. It's way past time for her owners to claim her."

"They shouldn't be allowed to get her back . . ."

Sinclair sticks his fingers through the fence and Beauty licks them.

"Well, you know, she was their property. If they'd come for her we'd have had to turn her over."

"That makes me sick!"

"Well . . . they're *not* claiming her, so we don't need to worry about that. And she'll make a great pet for someone."

Lots of animals I've been very attached to have been adopted out. That's the goal here. But Beauty? I'd never even considered the possibility.

One thing I know, my mom would never go for another dog. I've tried that before.

On the way home, Sinclair tells me about his niece who went into a deep depression after she'd had an abortion.

"*I* haven't had an abortion, if that's what you're thinking."

"Well then, how about this . . ."

And he tells me about how difficult it was for his friend in high school to admit she was a lesbian, even to herself.

"Actually, it was an awful time in *my* life, when I was trying to accept that I was different from the man my parents thought they'd raised. I was so tired of living in the closet—living a lie, and scared to death to come out."

"It's not that, either," I say.

"Well, then, is it AIDS, is it pregnancy, is it drugs, is it parental divorce, is it worry over school, is it . . . "

"Stop!" I say, smiling.

"Hangnails, ingrown toenails, pimples or pox?"

When he lets me out, Sinclair says, "Seriously, if you want to talk I'll listen. Life can be so hard sometimes . . ."

"Thanks," I say, getting my keys out and waving to him from the porch.

Mom and Dad are just opening cartons of Chinese food.

"Some of your favorites," Dad says. "Come eat with us."

I wash my hands at the sink and sit down.

"Where's Rocky?"

"Spending the night at Gramma's," Mom smiles. "That's how we can get away with eating Chinese and not having to listen to her whine."

As much as the three of us like Chinese food, our dinner together feels somehow tense and tasteless. It doesn't surprise me when, after I've set my fork on my empty plate, Dad tells me that he and Mom want to talk with me.

Man oh man, it seems like everyone has chosen tonight to want to talk with me. First Danny, then Sinclair, and now my parents.

"Have you thought about what you'll do if you turn up pregnant?" Dad says.

Nothing like coming straight to the point, I guess.

"Mostly I just think I'll figure that out when the time comes."

"When do you think the time will come?" Mom asks.

I look at Mom questioningly.

"Well . . . are you late?"

"A little. But they told me at the hospital that it wasn't uncommon even to skip a period, or lots of periods, after a rape."

"I'm sure that's true. I just wonder if you've given it any thought."

"Well . . . I'd probably have an abortion. I mean, Joey's baby?"

"I hope that's what you'd decide," Dad says, studying the pattern on his dinner plate.

"Or, adoption, if you'd have bad feelings about an abortion," Mom says.

I sigh. "You know, I really would rather not think about this unless I have to."

"Well . . . we're just worried about you, Erica. You seem so withdrawn . . ."

"Your mother and I thought it might be a good idea just to talk about all of the possibilities . . . "

"Dad . . . "

"Okay, E.J. Okay. Just don't shut us out."

"I won't. I'm trying not to," I say, giving each of them a kiss on the cheek and then going into the bathroom to run the water for the scalding hot bath I've been taking every morning and every night since Joey made me so dirty.

I've got a lot on my mind. My time is late, and I'm never late. I know what they said at the hospital, about it being pretty common to have your whole cycle messed up after a rape, but what if I *am* pregnant? God. I don't want Joey's baby! I don't want any baby, but the idea of having a baby with Joey's genetic make-up? No way do I want to add any more of those genes to the next generation!

And then there's the AIDS test. HIV they call it, but what's the difference? If you're HIV positive, eventually you get AIDS. And the hearing is coming up. I dread testifying at the hearing. I thought I'd have a choice, like if we dropped the charges then I wouldn't have to go through all that. But the lawyer told me that because Joey's on parole I could get subpoenaed anyway. And then, after the hearing, maybe there'll be a trial.

I want Joey to stay locked up but I get all sweaty just thinking about being placed on the witness stand and having to testify in public, and then being asked all kinds of embarrassing questions by a defense lawyer. It doesn't seem fair—first there's the horrible experience of being raped, and then there's another horrible experience of a trial. But what can I do? I've always had plans and goals, but right now I'm sort of doing that one day at a time thing.

And speaking of plans and goals, I'm so far behind in school it scares me to even think about it. And another thing I'm scared to think about is Beauty's going to be adopted out.

Things are weird at home, too. My parents are always watching me. My mom and dad are always totally serious, and sort of sad, all the time. My dad, who was such a big joker, hardly ever jokes around anymore. On the other hand, Rochelle hardly ever even looks at me, and when she does, it's like I'm a stranger. I know she was scared to death that night, as scared as I was, I guess. But now it's like I'm invisible, or something. I don't know which is worse, feeling invisible, or feeling like I'm being watched all the time.

It's weird at school, too. I feel like *everyone* is watching me, knowing I've been raped, whispering. April says no one even knows, and that I'm being too sensitive. It seems like I'm either too sensitive to everything around me, or I'm numb living somewhere out on Pluto. I can't find a balance.

On the day before the hearing, where April, Rocky and I will all have to testify, I'm so nervous I can't even think right. A lawyer from the district attorney's office has talked with us about every detail of that night with Joey. He's told us what to expect from the defense lawyer and even had us practice answering questions.

Some of the questions get me really angry, like didn't I always secretly wish Joey was my boyfriend, and wasn't I wearing something that would reasonably cause Joey to think I wanted sex—questions that could make the virgin Mary sound like a slut. No wonder I'm all shaky.

It's bad enough we had to go through all that stuff in the D.A.'s office. Now we have to say it all again at the hearing, in a courtroom, in front of a bunch of people, including Joey. I don't want to do it, but I can't figure a way out. April says she'll just pretend she's an actress in a movie, but I'm not sure I can do that. Lately I've had a hard time floating overhead, staying detached. Lately I've had to live with myself—no escape.

Almost everyone is gone from the Humane Society. Sinclair is still in his office upstairs, and the caretaker is in his apartment across the alley from the back parking lot. The night-shift officers are out in their trucks. I check on a cat that was spayed this morning. It is quiet tonight in the infirmary, orderly and clean.

I stand facing the locked double doors that lead to the off-limits area. I know where the keys are kept. I know how to mix the solution based on an animal's weight. I know it would be quick and painless. No hearings. No late periods. No HIV tests. No eyes watching, voices whispering, none of that, no more for me. Ten steps away, the keys are in the can that looks like furniture polish, in the bottom drawer of Dr. Franz's desk. Dazed, motionless, I stand, staring at the locks on the doors, imagining a timeless peace.

I'm roused by a frantic barking, different than the barking that is always background for my work here. This is trouble barking, hurt barking. I run to the kennels and see Beauty, struggling to get through the fence, yelping, howling, making sounds I've never heard come from any dog before. All the other dogs are stirred now, adding their own racket to the clamor of the night.

As soon as Beauty sees me, she lies down, resting her head on her paws, suddenly calm. Sinclair stands looking down from the balcony outside his office.

"*What* was *that* about?"

"I have no idea," I say, reaching through the gate and petting Beauty. She licks my hand and wags her tail. Her coat is thick now— no more mange or bare spots.

"Everything okay in there?" the caretaker calls through the back gate.

"I guess so," Sinclair says.

I sign out and go home. Rochelle is on the phone to Jessica, giggling. My mom is at the desk paying bills, and my dad is washing the dinner dishes. I imagine for a moment how this scene would have changed with a phone call announcing my death, requesting that one of them identify my body, the sorrow and confusion that would have surrounded their memories of me. I apologize silently to my unknowing family—I'm sorry for even thinking such a thing.

W as it coincidence that Beauty caused such a commotion in the kennels just as I was being drawn to the double doors and oblivion?

Or did she sense something and reach out to me, as I had reached out to her when she was so close to giving up? Two dogs have saved my life, first Kitty, when she attacked Joey, and now Beauty.

In a flash of clarity I know I *will* become a vet. I'll get past the aftermath of the rape and the loss of dreams I shared with Danny. I'm not sure how, but I will.

20

We are sitting lined up on a bench, Mom, Dad, April, Rocky and I, outside the hearing room.

"You be Jody Foster and I'll be Kelly McGillis," April says to me on the morning of the hearing.

"I wanna be that girl on 'Flipper'," Rocky says. We all laugh in that nervous way people do when a room is filled with tension.

Gladys Kendall and Alex are sitting on a bench on the other side of the courtroom doors. Gladys is dressed in a dark pants suit with a light turtle-neck sweater, looking very sober and business-like. Alex is wearing a dress shirt and a tie. I suppose their lawyer told them how to dress, just as the D.A. made suggestions to us.

It is nerve-racking, just sitting here, waiting to be called inside, but that's what we're supposed to do. After about an hour of wasted time, I decide I could at least be studying.

"I want to get my books from the car," I tell Dad, holding my hand out for the keys.

"Hurry," he says, handing them to me.

I'm halfway to the car when I hear footsteps behind me and turn to see Alex.

"Wait up," he says.

When he catches up to me he says, "I know my mom tried to get you to drop charges."

I nod.

"I just want you to know I don't agree with her," he says.

"You don't?"

He closes his eyes and shakes his head, and I wonder if he is going to cry.

"My mom is blind when it comes to Joey, but I know . . . I know he's not a good person."

We are standing in the cold, in the parking lot, and I'm waiting to hear what's next.

"Something went wrong with Joey a long time ago. Maybe when my dad left. Or maybe he's always been that way. Even when we were little kids, I was afraid of him. He'd hurt people, just to do it . . . we had a cat . . ."

"Your mom thinks Joey didn't mean anything by what he did to me."

"God. Erica, when I heard . . . how awful for you . . . "

Alex is having a hard time talking.

"I . . . it wouldn't have happened if I'd been home, I swear."

We walk together to my parents' car. I get my books out and we walk slowly back toward the courthouse.

"Danny's quit drinking," Alex says.

"Good."

"We're not selling anymore, either. We were lucky we didn't get caught. Joey talked us into it, the small business plan, you know? We were stupid."

"I was pretty stupid, too," I say.

"You?"

"When I saw how drunk Danny was that night, I should have left then. None of this would have happened if I hadn't always been trying to take care of Danny instead of watching out for myself."

We get to the door and Alex touches my shoulder. "You're doing the right thing."

It is the right thing, I think, as I enter the courtroom and wait to take the stand. But it is not an easy thing, going over and over the details of being raped. It's like it will never be over.

The night after I testify, I wake up screaming, feeling it again, living it again. Mom and Dad both rush to my room. It takes me a moment to get calm, and then I tell them, "I'm okay—just a dream."

"You're not okay, Erica. I want you to call Jenny and get started with one of her groups."

"I don't see how that can help," I say.

"Maybe it can't, but it's worth a try."

The Rape Crisis Center occupies space in the old YWCA building. The room where Jenny's group meets has high ceilings and windows that are so tall they can't be opened or closed without using a long pole. There is a cart of coffee, tea, and cookies setting in the corner. Counting Jenny, there are nine of us sitting in mostly worn-out upholstered chairs that have been arranged in a circle.

Only girls and women sit in this room at the Rape Crisis Center. Women, Jenny calls us, but I don't feel grown-up right now, and I doubt that the twelve-year-old sitting next to Jenny does either. There are three African American women, three who I guess to be Mexican, counting me, and one Asian and two white. Not that it matters. I just notice those things.

When it is my turn to introduce myself I say, "My name is Erica—I'm only here because my mom kept nagging me to come."

The woman next to me, Jewel, turns to me angrily. "The first thing you better figure out is what *you* want, not what someone else wants."

"How long did that take you, Jewel?" an older woman sitting across from us asks softly.

Jewel flashes her a look, then lets out a raucous laugh. "About thirty years."

"How old are you?"

"Twenty-nine," Jewel says.

Everyone laughs and the tension lifts.

"Maybe saying you're here because of your mother is only an excuse to do what you want to do, anyway," Kendra says.

Maybe so, I think, but I don't say it.

Gradually, over a period of weeks, I learn about the women in the rape survivors support group. Most of their stories are worse than mine—the twelve-year-old was raped by her older brother, Jewel was gang raped at a party, another woman was raped repeatedly by her own husband, once in front of a neighbor. But we don't just stay stuck on the bad stuff. We talk about what makes us stronger, too.

One of the things the support group helped me out with is how to deal with flashbacks. Like yesterday. I ran a comb through my hair and noticed it's longer—almost long enough now to grab hold of. Suddenly I could feel Joey's hand grabbing, pulling my head back. I smelled his whiskey breath, as if it were happening all over again. I took three deep breaths and repeated to myself, it's over, it's over. And then it *was* over, and I went on with what I was doing. I learned that in the group: Breathe deep, know it's over. Let it pass. It's over.

The group helps in other ways too. Knowing other survivors helps. Thinking of ourselves as survivors rather than victims also helps.

In February, the day before Washington's birthday, I call the clinic to get the results of my HIV test. I get put on hold so I hang up. What if I've tested positive? Maybe it's better not to know. But I've got to know. I press redial. I give the person at the test results extension my secret identification number.

She puts me on hold. This time I wait, breathless.

"Negative," she says.

"Thanks."

I call April, and Mom, at work, and tell them the news.

"When do you have to be tested again?"

"Six months. Every six months for two years."

"It wouldn't surprise me if that scum bag Joey has HIV," April says.

"Thanks for the reassurance."

"I'm sorry. But really, don't you just know that creep's done every drug in the book and had sex under the very worst possible conditions?"

"No, I don't know that. I suppose it's possible though."

"Anyway, you tested negative, that's all that matters."

"It could still be in the incubation period," I say, "but I'm relieved, anyway."

"Me, too," April says. "Remember I drank from your soda bottle last week."

We laugh. There's a kind of airhead girl in Peer Counseling who insists she knows someone who got HIV from drinking from a friend's soda bottle. No amount of scientific information will change her opinion. She's one of those people whose motto is "Don't confuse me with the facts."

Things are looking up for me because Washington's birthday, the day after I got my test results, I finally get my period.

"Yea!" I scream.

Mom comes running into the bathroom.

"What is it?"

I know this sounds totally gross, but I show her the wad of toilet paper smeared with blood. She looks at me blankly at first, then throws her arms around me.

"I'm so glad you don't have to deal with a pregnancy," she says. "So glad!"

Rocky comes in to see what's going on. "Is it today you are a woman?" she asks, all smart alecky.

"Just because you've read a booklet from the Kotex Company doesn't mean you know everything," I say.

We all laugh, and I feel a lightness I've not felt in a long time.

When Dad gets back from the hardware store Mom tells him, "Good news—she fell off the roof."

I don't know where my mom comes up with these sayings, but Dad understands immediately. He picks me up and twirls me around.

"Let's celebrate," he says. "I can replace light fixtures any day."

We all pile into the car, Kitty included. We stop at the Grains and Greens market and get salads, bread, drinks, paper plates—everything we need for a picnic, and then drive to Griffith Park. I attach the leash to Kitty's collar, and we find a spot on the side of a hill that's not too crowded.

"The joys of Southern California," Dad says, stretching out on our giant picnic blanket. "Picnics in February."

"It beats Germany, doesn't it?" Mom says.

"Yep. In fact, I think I'm not even going back to Germany! I'll just *stay* in Southern California."

We all stop what we're doing and look at Dad. Can he be serious?

"I need final approval, but I've requested a change of duty—I can work in recruiting, in Los Angeles, for the next two years and then retire."

"A desk job?" Mom says, raising her eyebrows. "I thought you'd never take a desk job."

Dad looks from one to the other of us. "It's worth it to be home. The trial's coming up . . . I don't want to be overseas while you're all going through that . . . "

Mom sits down on the blanket next to Dad. She looks him in the eye, holding his gaze for what seems a long time.

"I didn't even know you were considering such a change."

"Well . . . I wanted to be sure it could happen before I got us all stirred up about the possibility of a normal life," he smiles.

Rocky, never one to be slow about seizing an opportunity, says, "Will you help coach my softball team?"

"We'll see," Dad says.

"Are you sure about this?" Mom asks.

"I guess they *could* say no—I was going to wait until I got the final signed papers to tell you. But I'm ninety-nine percent sure they won't say no."

Mom puts her arms around Dad and leans into his chest. "I can hardly believe it," she says.

"I know—a totally different life than any we've ever had. Even when we were all living together on army bases I was out on maneuvers half the time."

Dad strokes Mom's head. "Can you stand to have me around all the time?" he asks.

"It'll take some getting used to," she laughs, hugging him.

I watch, wondering about love. It seemed like Danny and I had so much together, but—I don't know. Was it all in my head? Just wishes and dreams and no reality? Sometimes I wonder if I will ever in my whole life find a real love. And how will I know? I was so sure with Danny. How can I ever be sure again? And I wonder if I'll ever want to have sex again.

We talk a lot in the survivors group about what being raped has done to us in relation to a normal sex life. One woman, Tanya, says she has sex with practically every guy she meets now. She says if you get raped by one man, and you've had sex with three men in your life, that means 25 percent of the men you've been with have raped you, and that's a frightening statistic. But if you get raped by one man, and you have sex with one hundred others, you've only got a one percent rape history. Tanya says one percent is manageable.

I don't think any percentage is manageable when it comes to rape, but we all deal with things in our own way. For now, I'm a born-again virgin. I don't know if that's for life or not. I guess I'll figure that out later on.

I take Kitty's leash and start off walking. Rocky catches up. We walk farther into the hills, away from traffic noises. In the distance we can see the planetarium.

"Do you think there's life on other planets?" Rocky says.

"Maybe."

"I'm sure there is."

"How do you know?"

"I just know. And I'm going to Mars someday, too."

"Well . . . why not?" I say.

She grins at me. "I haven't told anyone else yet."

"Okay. I won't tell yet, either."

We sit down near the top of the hill.

"Kitty's hair's almost grown back," Rocky says.

"But look, you can see the scar," I tell her, separating strands of hair on Kitty's neck and showing Rocky the jagged line of raised, pink skin.

"I hate that Joey guy," Rocky says, narrowing her eyes and frowning. Then she jumps up, takes the leash, and starts running downhill with Kitty.

I follow after them, no longer worried about being invisible to Rocky, or worse, like I'm some kind of repulsive beetle as far as she's concerned. I catch up with them and race them back to the blanket where Mom and Dad sit close to each other, talking.

I don't really believe that saying about how everything comes in threes. All you have to do is be able to divide by three and you can look at everything that way. Five deaths in the family? The first three prove the groups of three thing, and the last two will become three as soon as the next person dies. *But*, after getting the two pieces of great news, I'm HIV negative and I'm not pregnant, another great piece of news is waiting for me when I get to the Humane Society Tuesday afternoon.

I go to Beauty's cage first, like always, and I see in bold letters, stamped across her card, ADOPTED. My heart sinks. I may never see her again. What kind of people are adopting her? I run into the adoption office and check the computer. It takes forever to warm up, and then I can't find the new adoptions file. Finally, my fingers find the right keys and the computer does its thing. There it is—Beauty, Female, Border Collie mix—adopter—Sinclair Manchester. I am so happy I start laughing, all by myself in the little office. I run upstairs.

"Sinclair!"

"Yes, love," he says, looking up from his neatly drawn charts.

"You're taking Beauty!"

"Hello, Hello." The parrot jumps from one perch to another, then grabs hold of its cage with its crooked beak.

"Ummm. I decided it was the next best thing to you taking her, and I understand how your mom feels about two dogs. Besides, you're going off to college in August."

I throw my arms around Sinclair. He hugs me, quick, then pushes me away.

"Don't wrinkle me," he says, smoothing the front of his shirt. Then he tells me about a family who came looking for a dog yesterday, and the dog they liked best was Beauty. They said they'd be back, but they didn't put in an official request.

"So I moved fast," he says. "I figure, she can hang out here in the daytime, in the office, or downstairs, and then I'll take her home with me at night. Good idea?"

"Great idea!" I say.

Sinclair laughs. "Is this the pre-Christmas Erica I see?"

"I'll never be pre-Christmas again," I tell him. "But I'll be happy."

"That's the spirit," Sinclair says.

21

For the first time in my life, I don't care about school. I go through the motions—attending class, carrying my notebook, but I can't get interested in studying, or homework, or tests. It's like my life is on hold and I don't know how to punch the button and take the call. Then, in March, I get a letter of acceptance from UC Davis, and something kicks in.

"I'm going to Davis—animal husbandry," I yell when I open the envelope.

The trouble is, when I read the fine print I see that my acceptance is based on the expectation that my final semester grades will be as good as my previous record. Yikes! I start hustling to get my grades up.

I talk with each of my teachers, explaining I've had a hard time, without going into the gory details, and asking if there's any way I can pull my *B*s and *C*s back up to *A*s. It turns out there is a way, and it's to eat, breathe, and sleep school. I cut back on my hours at the Humane Society and immerse myself in the game of academic catch-up.

I'm studying, as usual, one night, when Danny calls. Rocky answers the phone and comes running in with it.

"Hi," Danny says.

"Hi."

"Did you get the news yet?"

"What news?"

"Joey did a plea bargain thing—pled guilty to assault. It's a shorter sentence, but it's still going to be tough on him because of being on parole . . . But no trial, unless you demand it."

It takes awhile for me to process what Danny's just said.

"What's his sentence?"

"I don't know. Years."

"And no trial?"

"Unless you demand one."

Tears of relief gather in my eyes.

"I knew you'd want to know right away," Danny says.

"Thanks."

"I'm doing better, Erica. I'm working at True Value Hardware, and I'm hardly drinking at all."

"I'm doing better, too."

"Well . . . do you want to go to a movie or anything sometime?"

"No. Not yet."

"But sometime?"

"I don't know, Danny. Right now, it doesn't seem like it."

"I won't always be waiting."

"I'm not asking you to wait."

"Well, 'bye."

"'Bye," I say.

In the morning Dad calls the D.A.'s office and they confirm Danny's story. Finally, it's as if I can breathe freely for the first time since Christmas, like a giant weight has been lifted from my chest.

I end up with a 3.6 grade point average for my last semester at Hamilton High School. Not bad, but not good enough for Davis, especially not for the Animal Husbandry program. But Dr. Franz writes a letter to the head of that department, someone she used to be on some committee with, and she mentions extenuating circumstances and then goes on to say what great potential I have for the field of veterinary medicine. I hardly recognize myself when she shows it to me to read—all five pages of it.

"This is all the truth," she says, folding the letter, addressing an envelope, and sealing it.

I can feel my face getting hot.

"Really," she says.

By mid-June I've got all kinds of forms to fill out for Davis. They even ask what kind of music I like to listen to, and if I like it loud or soft. I guess they're trying to get compatible roommates.

In July, I get my second HIV test, and it comes back negative. I think I'm okay. I'll have to get tested again in another six months, though.

The night before I leave for Davis, April and I go to the Mean Bean, which is a coffee place in Old Town. We sit at a table with a checkerboard and play checkers, barely paying attention to what we're doing.

"It's going to be so strange with you gone," she says. "I still can't believe we won't be going back to good old Hamilton High in September."

I jump April's king.

"No fair, you were watching the game," she says.

We laugh. "I wish you were going with me," I tell her.

"Yeah," she sighs. "I'm going to come see you in about a month—hang out for a week. That'll be the best way to go to Davis. No studying."

We laugh. "You're the best friend I've ever had," I tell her. Then I jump her other king.

"Some friend." She laughs harder, then throws her napkin at me.

The yuppie couple sitting at the next table both turn and give us disgusted looks. We laugh harder, then April gets all serious.

"Guess who I saw earlier this afternoon, before I came to get you?"

"Sean Penn?"

"No."

I wait.

"Danny Lara. At first I wasn't sure I should tell you, but we always tell each other everything, right?"

"Right."

"So, do you want to know?"

"How do I know if I want to know until I know?"

"But then it's too late," April says.

"Just tell me. You're going to tell me anyway."

"Well, I saw Danny walking out of Barb and Edie's, and he was with that girl who used to ride the same bus with us when we were sophomores. You know, Lisa."

"Lisa Riley?"

"Yeah, and it's weird. She looks exactly like you. Or at least like you looked before you cut all your hair off—they were holding hands."

"It's a free country," I say, wondering why I have a funny feeling in my stomach when I've hardly even seen Danny all summer long.

"But don't you think it's creepy? That he's chosen your clone? Well, not in the brains department she's not your clone, but in the looks department—twins."

I'm all cool, talking with April like I couldn't care less that Danny's found someone else. But inside I've got butterflies.

"What do you care? You're going to find some studly college man who's your intellectual peer."

"I'm not looking," I tell April. "I'm sticking with my born-again status."

"But if Mr. Right comes along?"

"When I'm thirty. What about you? Don't you ever miss what you had with Wade?"

"Hey! Wade was no winner. What's to miss? I'm waiting for Sean Penn to notice me."

That gets us laughing again, and the yuppies are annoyed again, so we pay our bill and leave.

When I get home my dad tells me I'd better be sure everything's ready to go. He wants to be on the road to UC Davis by seven in the morning.

"Really, six would be better," he says. "It'll be unbearably hot going up I-5."

"But we have air conditioning, don't we?" Rocky whines.

Because of all the stuff I have to take—books, linens, clothes, of course, and tapes and CDs—my dad has rented a van just for the trip.

"Even so, we'll be more comfortable if we get an early start. That's for sure."

In spite of Dad's hopes for an early start, it is nearly eight by the time everything is packed in the van and we're all ready to go. He and Mom sit in front. Rocky gets the seat behind them all to herself, and Kitty and I take the back seat. We stop at Gramma's so I can say good-bye.

I get out and run up to the door.

"Erica! I can't believe you're so grown-up," she says, misty-eyed.

I give her a big hug. "I'll write to you."

"Just call collect," she says.

We talk for a minute and then Dad taps the horn.

"Don't get bossy with me!" she yells at him, laughing. He shakes his head in that "what can I do with her" kind of way.

"I have something for you," Gramma says.

I follow her inside and there, sitting on top of the TV, are my old slippers.

"You might need them," she says with an impish grin.

I take them from the TV, not knowing what to say. Dad honks the horn again.

"'Bye, Gramma," I say, giving her a quick hug and running out the door. I get in the van, in the far back, next to Kitty, and slam the heavy, sliding door.

As we back out the driveway and into the street, Gramma stands on the steps, waving good-bye, laughing.

Just past Coalinga, which Dad says is the half-way mark, I slip my bare feet into the slippers. I know they're a bit small, but this is ridiculous. I can barely get my toes in. I reach inside to see what's in the way. A packet of three condoms. In the other slipper is a can of foam and a folded paper. When I unfold the paper a one hundred dollar bill is sitting on top of a note.

Dear Erica,

*I hope you won't need this. As you know, the best protection is abstinence and sex is meant for marriage, not for fooling around. But, better safe than sorry I always say. I **know** you can use the money. My love and best wishes follow you wherever you go.*

Gramma

I tuck Gramma's gifts into my backpack, smiling. I'm glad she did that. We never even talked about what she found in my slippers that day, and it was like there was something strained between us. Not a big strain. A little one. But no more.

I lean over next to Kitty, lay my head against her back and drift somewhere between waking and sleeping. I'll miss her so much, my life-saver dog, and Beauty, too, and my family, and April, and Sinclair and Dr. Franz. But I'm way excited about a new life.

I think I won't use Gramma's presents to me within their expiration date. I'm not anti-men or anything, like some of the women in my rape survivors group are. There's a lot I'm still uncertain about, though. But I *am* certain I'll be a vet. And I'm also certain that if I ever take another chance on love, I won't get so caught up in someone else's problems that I lose sight of the kind of person *I* want to be.

Kitty groans and stretches full out in the seat, pushing me off to the side. I sit up, groggy.

"But what about me?" I say, moving her gently but firmly back to her own side.

In the front seat Mom and Dad latch onto my words with some old seventies song, "Hey, ey, ey, ey, ey, ey, what about me. I've got a song that I can sing, too."

I lie back down and close my eyes, imagining the buildings I've seen in the Davis brochure, and wondering what kind of music my roommate *will* like. I hope it's not Ian and Sylvia or The Honey Drippers. That's okay for my mom and dad, but I wouldn't like a steady diet of it.

What if I don't find any friends? What if the work's too hard?
What if I get miserably homesick . . . Why am I worrying about
things that probably won't even happen? And if they do, I know I'll
handle it.

I already know I can get through hard times. I have. I will again,
if I need to. But good times are ahead. I feel it as strongly as I feel
Kitty pushing at me, trying to hog (or is it dog?) the whole seat.

ABOUT
THE AUTHOR

In addition to *But What About Me?* Marilyn Reynolds is the author of three other young adult novels, *Too Soon for Jeff, Detour for Emmy,* and *Telling,* and a book of short stories, *Beyond Dreams,* all part of the popular **True-to-Life Series from Hamilton High.**

According to *Booklist, Too Soon for Jeff* is a teen father's story which is "a thoughtful book for both young men and young women." This novel has been adapted for an ABC After-School Special, scheduled to air September 12, 1996.

Detour for Emmy, a teen mother's story which *Kliatt* described as "honest, heart-wrenching, inspirational, informative," won the 1995-1996 South Carolina Young Adult Book Award. Both *Too Soon for Jeff* and *Detour for Emmy* were selected by the American Library Association for its Best Books for Young Adults list, and these two books, plus *Telling* and *Beyond Dreams,* have been selected for the New York Public Library's list of **Books for the Teen-Age Reader.**

Reviewing the short stories in *Beyond Dreams, Booklist* states, "All the young people are believable, likeable, and appropriately thoughtful . . . the stories are interesting and well paced . . ."

Of *Telling,* a story in which twelve-year-old Cassie is

being molested by a neighbor, *School Library Journal* states, "Reynolds has done a superb job of weaving the complexities of difficult issues into the life of an innocent child."

In addition to writing, Reynolds continues to work with students at Century High School, and to seek their insights on early drafts of her stories. She balances her time between writing, working with high school students, and keeping her backyard bird feeder filled. Her students help her keep in touch with the realities of today's teens, realities which are readily apparent in her novels.

She lives in Southern California with her husband, Mike. They are the parents of three grown children, Sharon, Cindi, and Matt, and the grandparents of Ashley, Kerry, and Subei.

OTHER RESOURCES FROM MORNING GLORY PRESS

DETOUR FOR EMMY. Novel about teenage pregnancy by Reynolds.

TOO SOON FOR JEFF. Novel from teen father's perspective. By Marilyn Reynolds.

TELLING. Novel about sexual molestation of 12-year-old. Reynolds.

BEYOND DREAMS. Six short stories about crises faced by teens.

WILL THE DOLLARS STRETCH? Four short stories about teen parents moving out on their own. Includes check register exercises.

TEENAGE COUPLES—Caring, Commitment and Change: How to Build a Relationship that Lasts. TEENAGE COUPLES— Coping with Reality: Dealing with Money, In-Laws, Babies and Other Details of Daily Life. Help teen couples develop healthy, loving, relationships.

TEENAGE COUPLES—EXPECTATIONS AND REALITY. For professionals, research results of survey of teenage couples.

TEENS PARENTING—Your Pregnancy and Newborn Journey
How to take care of yourself and your newborn. For pregnant teens. Available in "regular" (RL 6), Easier Reading (RL 3), and Spanish.

TEENS PARENTING—Your Baby's First Year
TEENS PARENTING—The Challenge of Toddlers
TEENS PARENTING—Discipline from Birth to Three.
Three how-to-parent books especially for teenage parents.

VIDEOS: "Discipline from Birth to Three" and "Your Baby's First Year" supplements above books.

TEEN DADS: Rights, Responsibilities and Joys. Parenting book for teenage fathers.

SURVIVING TEEN PREGNANCY: Choices, Dreams, Decisions
For all pregnant teens—help with decisions, moving on toward goals.

SCHOOL-AGE PARENTS: The Challenge of Three-Generation Living. Help for families when teen daughter (or son) has a child.

BREAKING FREE FROM PARTNER ABUSE. Guidance for victims of domestic violence.

DID MY FIRST MOTHER LOVE ME? A Story for an Adopted Child. Birthmother shares her reasons for placing her child.

DO I HAVE A DADDY? A Story About a Single-Parent Child
Picture/story book especially for children with only one parent. Also available in Spanish, *¿Yo tengo papá?*

MORNING GLORY PRESS

6595 San Haroldo Way, Buena Park, CA 90620
714/828-1998 — FAX 714/828-2049

Please send me the following: Price   Total

___*But What About Me?*	Paper, ISBN 1-885356-10-2	8.95	_____
___	Cloth, ISBN 1-885356-11-0	15.95	_____
___*Beyond Dreams*	Paper, ISBN 1-885356-00-5	8.95	_____
___	Cloth, ISBN 1-885356-01-3	15.95	_____
___*Too Soon for Jeff*	Paper, ISBN 0-930934-91-1	8.95	_____
___	Cloth, ISBN 0-930934-90-3	15.95	_____
___*Detour for Emmy*	Paper, ISBN 0-930934-76-8	8.95	_____
___	Cloth, ISBN 0-930934-75-x	15.95	_____
___*Telling*	Paper, ISBN 1-885356-03-x	8.95	_____
___	Cloth, ISBN 1-885356-04-8	15.95	_____
___*Will the Dollars Stretch?*	Paper, ISBN 1-885356-12-9	6.95	_____
Teenage Couples: Expectations and Reality			
___	Paper, ISBN 0-930934-98-9	14.95	_____
___	Cloth, ISBN 0-930934-99-7	21.95	_____
Teenage Couples: Caring, Commitment and Change			
___	Paper, ISBN 0-930934-93-8	9.95	_____
___	Cloth, ISBN 0-930934-92-x	15.95	_____
Teenage Couples: Coping with Reality			
___	Paper, ISBN 0-930934-86-5	9.95	_____
___	Cloth, ISBN 0-930934-87-3	15.95	_____
___*Teen Dads*	Paper, ISBN 0-930934-78-4	9.95	_____
___*Do I Have a Daddy?*	Cloth, ISBN 0-930934-45-8	12.95	_____
___*Breaking Free from Partner Abuse* 0-930934-74-1		7.95	_____
___*Surviving Teen Pregnancy* Paper, 1-885356-06-4		11.95	_____
Teens Parenting—Your Pregnancy and Newborn Journey			
___	Paper, ISBN 0-930934-50-4	9.95	_____
Teens Parenting—Your Baby's First Year			
___	Paper, ISBN 0-930934-52-0	9.95	_____
Teens Parenting—Challenge of Toddlers			
___	Paper, ISBN 0-930934-58-x	9.95	_____
Teens Parenting—Discipline from Birth to Three			
___	Paper, ISBN 0-930934-54-7	9.95	_____
___**VIDEO: "Discipline from Birth to Three"**		195.00	_____
___**VIDEO: "Your Baby's First Year"**		195.00	_____

TOTAL _____

Please add postage: 10% of total—Min., $3.00   _____
California residents add 7.75% sales tax   _____

TOTAL _____

Ask about quantity discounts, Teacher, Student Guides.
Prepayment requested. School/library purchase orders accepted.
If not satisfied, return in 15 days for refund.

NAME _____

ADDRESS_____

_____